Deadly Epiphany

By

Kareen Martin

ISBN-13:
978-1530573592

ISBN-10:
1530573599

3rd November, 1966

Zach hated school, especially when it was his birthday. Today he was fourteen years old. This morning, before she left the house, his mother had given him a present of a knitted jumper and a second-hand pencil case, wrapped in yesterday's newspaper. His father, waking in one of his moods again, had walked into the kitchen, giving him a resounding clip around the head as he passed.

They both left for work together, leaving Zach sitting alone at the kitchen table with a plate of bread and margarine for his breakfast. As soon as he heard the back gate slam shut, he threw his breakfast out for the birds. His dad was a builder but his mum worked in the town's toilets and everything in his house, including his food, stank of piss. Zach was sure his mother never washed her hands, even after they'd spent most of the day down toilet bowls, clearing up other people's shit. He peered through the grimy window and as soon as the coast was clear, he left his home.

On arriving at school he went straight to his classroom, preferring not to join the other boys and girls in the playground. Today was Thursday, and in Zach's poor life, it had become the most special day of the week. Normally, he would have the classroom to himself for about half an hour, but today Miss Bats, as he called her, interrupted him in his work. He ducked down behind his desk, hoping he hadn't been seen and waited apprehensively. After a while he peeked over the desk. Bats still sat there, writing at her table. It was so quiet in the room; you could hear her breathing and the scrape of pen against paper.

Just then the door creaked open. A tall, skinny lad entered. It was Ian Peaceful. "What do you want, boy?" Bats shouted.

Zack couldn't see him but he recognised the gasp and the cowering whisper. "Nothing, Miss," the boy whimpered.

"Out now," Bats ordered. The boy scarpered. Zach heard the sound of a drawer being slammed shut. Then he heard

Miss Bats leave the room and he cautiously lifted his head.

"All clear," he muttered to himself and sidled to the front of the classroom. His eyes darting back and forth towards the door, he carefully slid open the desk drawer. He saw the note, scrunched up and shoved towards the back, and pulled it out. Smoothing the creases, he hurriedly read the words. His eyes gleamed and he grinned. Well, well, he gloated to himself. Who would have thought? He put the note in his pocket and watched the door expectantly.

A couple of minutes later the door slowly opened. The same lad appeared, first his head, then the rest of him. He closed the door behind him and flattened his back against the door. He stared at Zach fearfully. His voice shook as he asked. "Have you got my money?"

"Say please," Zach ordered.

"Please," grovelled the boy. "I did everything you asked."

Zach's eyes raked over the pathetic figure. Although a little older, Ian was such a wimp. A right scaredy-cat. It made him feel so powerful, having such a snivelling creature at his beck and call. Zach's elder brother, Ted, now living in some godforsaken prison in the middle of Dartmoor, had taught him well. How to pick your victim had been a valuable lesson for him. Ted had told him you could smell fear and he'd been right. The boy in front of him reeked of the stuff. Zach smiled nastily. There were other boys as well, waiting to be paid their dues, but he enjoyed teasing this boy the most.

He put in hand in his back pocket and pulled out a handful of change. He held it out, forcing the boy to walk towards him.

"I've got another little job for you," he said. "Come and see me later."

The assorted coins were snatched from his hand. Ian eyed them greedily. "Okay," he said and slipped out of the room.

Zach waited for the next one. Thursdays were such a busy day.

Chapter One

Percy Crouch watched the early morning mist that had crept insidiously through the night roll gently over the cliffs and gradually evaporate under the warmth of the rising sun. The Jurassic landscape gently unveiled itself. Diamonds, millions of them, dancing in the sea and dew-laden cobwebs glittering on the leaves and hedgerows as far as the eye could see. Birds, long-risen, sang excitedly in the trees, and rabbits, squirrels, and all manner of creatures darted in and out of the undergrowth. Nature hummed, buzzed and chirped itself into the new day.

Percy stood alone on the hilltop and stared up into the brightening sky and then across to the sea on his left. His gaze then shifted over the land that had been in his family for generations, his eyes watching the process of life with a deep melancholy. Today he found no solace in his surroundings. No peace. Only a pervading sense of menace.

He scored a shaking, wrinkled hand through his grey hair, catching several fine strands with his jagged nails. His lacklustre green eyes stared out from a round and liver-spotted face. Old, tired skin sagged around the jowls and folded into several chins. Running a farm with its early mornings and constant hard, unrelenting toil aged a man. He was barely fifty, yet today he felt like a hundred years old. The agony of his thoughts tormented him.

Farmer Percy Crouch wondered over and over again, what it would be like to kill a man. What it would be like to plunge a pitchfork deep into the flabby body or run him over with a tractor. Maybe a shot gun or a crack over the head with a pick axe? Knives? Poison? On a farm there were so many implements of death he was spoilt for choice.

Could he do it though? Killing farm animals was one thing. Killing another human being? His breath staggered in his throat. Could he, a God-fearing man, actually commit the ultimate sin? Murder. The will was there, the motive was strong and the anger had been simmering for months deep inside him. He stared into the distance and pin-pointed his son Ben, working in the top field. The lad was man-handling bales of hay with an ease born of practice and stacking them high in a pyramid-like formation. This was what spurred Percy Crouch on. It was for Ben's sake that he would have to kill.

He settled himself comfortably against the slats of the wooden gate and folded his arms across his round belly. He stared over his land, a land that had been in his family for four hundred years. As both man and boy he had sat in this very spot, proud to be the keeper and proud that one day, in the near future, he would hand over the running of the farm to his son, just as his father had done and many generations of fathers before him.

It was good land, full of hope and promise. The rising sun bounced off the newly cut fields turning them into shimmering ponds of gold. In contrast, the leaves of the silver maple trees, spinning in the soft breeze, glimmered, catching the light with every twist and turn. Sloping fields leading down to Badger Wood were a kaleidoscope of colour. Dandelions, daisies and multicoloured wild meadow flowers making a downy carpet. The smell of cattle and dung, flowers and cut hay mingling with a hint of ocean brine teased his nostrils. He spied a hawk, resting high on one of the telegraph poles that roped his land. It was as still as death, watching, waiting for one small creature to scurry out from the undergrowth. The hawk would pounce without remorse. He had to live, he had chicks to feed.

Percy Crouch felt like that hawk, standing alone, his fate in the hands of one small creature that inhabited his corner of the earth. Every living thing had a job to do. Each animal protecting its offspring so that the species could carry on. Just like he would safeguard his son. It was his and Ben's duty to carry on preserving their land, their heritage. Ben should have been next guardian.

Not now though. Ben had had his head turned with promises of bright lights, girls, money, and every technical gadget you could imagine. Luring him from his inheritance to a life he wouldn't be able to cope with. A simple boy, way out of his depth and all because of one small, greedy man with too much money. A man who believed he could buy everything he touched.

Well that wasn't going to happen. Words had failed. Threats had fallen on to deaf ears. The time for action had arrived. Today, Zach Allington had to die.

The Reverend Ian Peaceful also had murder on his mind that beautiful morning in August. It was later on in the day, almost noon and the sun was blazing down. The grass beneath his feet was brittle and snapped as he walked towards the bottom of the garden. The unexpected heatwave following a freezing spring had left the garden bedraggled and confused, the flowers, drooping and exhausted, the extensive lawn a dirty brown colour. Only the weeds seemed immune to the debilitating heat.

Could he do it, he asked himself for the hundredth time? Could he, a man of the cloth, murder his fellow man in cold blood? Yet what was the alternative? he wondered. The rest of his life living under a cloud of shame and remorse? Knowing eyes following him everywhere. He squeezed his eyes closed and shuddered. Absolute purgatory. The very idea, ludicrous and extreme, was unbearable. He pressed onwards, his hooked nose sniffing the air, sucking in what little breeze wafted by. He folded his full top lip over his lower fat lip and glowered with intense concentration towards the trees. Finally he took a deep breath and began walking purposely towards the beach.

As he broke through the gap in the trees, his feet touched a seam of sand, and he stopped again. Hesitating, he shoved his hands deep into the pockets of his black jeans. He felt, with calm reassurance, the touch of cold metal nestling within, dangerously silent. Everything was suddenly surreal to him. The soothing motion of the sea, the gentle rustling of the leaves yet his insides engulfed in a black, all consuming fear which spread stealthy like syrup through his veins.

He couldn't go on. The past with its dark shadows, its suspicious eyes and the here and now, meeting on this isolated beach, held him still. He prayed inwardly but knew that that was a fruitless diversion. He looked at his long spindly hands, their attitude one of affected prayer. Ridiculous, he scoffed to himself. He had shed his God along with his cassock many years before, and besides a thoroughly useless wife, he had no one. What he did have though, was a strong sense of self preservation, a secret promise lurking in the future and expectations concealed deep in his soul. To kill or be exposed for the fraud and defiler that he was? There was no contest. He knew from the day he met the rich and powerful Zach Allington again that the time would come when he would have murder in mind. That fateful day had arrived three days ago when the invitation had dropped innocently through the letterbox. 'The Revelation Party' it had said. Zach Allington had things to say. He was going to make a speech. He wanted to change lives.

Ian remembered Zach from school. The memories still had the power to fill him with helplessness. That hateful, slimy boy. The gatherer of people's darkest fears, who had rejoiced in the barbaric act of exploiting his victims' innermost desires. Ian had made a dreadful mistake one day. He'd allowed Zach to see right into his soul and from that moment, the boy first, then the man had persecuted him to the point of murder.

The Reverend wondered what Zach's wife Jenny felt about it. The poor woman was obviously devastated. He couldn't imagine how such an innocent woman had joined her life with such a foolish, vindictive bore. What kind of man exposes his wife and children to the ridicule of their friends? Jenny was so beautiful, so vulnerable, a stark contrast to his wife Muriel with her drab appearance and featureless face.

No, it was impossible to imagine how Jenny was feeling but he would help her all he could. He would protect her and protect himself.

He plunged onwards, stumbling slightly when he met the pebbles. Reaching the shoreline, the stagnant smell of rotting seaweed assaulted his nostrils. He looked to his left. Just around the corner, hidden from his eyes by a grey rocky cliff was his nemesis, the man who was about to die. He faltered again as he felt the cold steel of the weapon that lay dormant in his pocket. A feeling he'd never felt before made him shiver. For a moment he was terrified and swallowed hard to dispel the bile rising in his throat. He wasn't a religious man, not in his heart anyway and wondered, not for the first time, if he'd ever had been. Ian had been born into a God-fearing household, with parents who had used the Bible as a rule of life. God was thrust like a weapon on the family. To Ian, God was some nebulous creature who was there to blight his life, something to fear like monsters under the bed. And as he grew older the fear faded to be replaced by suspicion and disbelief. Now though, he fought off the insidious childhood fear creeping through his veins and tightened the grip on the handle of the weapon. *No... No*, a voice in his head cried. He shook inwardly. Was it his voice? he wondered. Was he being forced to deny his feelings? He could easily use it. He just had to be strong and ignore the voice that denied him retribution. He would make the death instantaneous and hopefully painless. After all, he thought, unlike Zach, he wasn't completely callous, he justified to himself.

The object of the Reverend's unwanted affections stood irresolutely at the bottom of the cliff on the opposite side of the beach. She watched with a confused frown on her forehead as Ian Peaceful reeled to and fro like a drunken man. He was having trouble walking, first on the sand, and then on the pebbles. Jenny wondered what he was doing on the beach in the midday heat but she stepped back behind the rocks and remained hidden. She did not want to be seen.

Right now, she needed solitude. Ian had become a bit

over-powering of late. A few kind words had become something more tactile, more uncomfortable and she had other issues that needed to be resolved first. Ian, with his unwelcome affections, would have to wait.

Zach was her first priority. What on earth had happened to the man? That stupid husband of hers wanted to give half their wealth away. He'd had a dream, a bloody epiphany for God's sake. Well that wasn't going to happen. She wasn't going to stand by and watch as he gave all their money away. The man was a complete fool, and after all she'd done! She gave a bitter laugh then clamped a hand over her mouth. "You fool," she muffled against her palm, her blue eyes darting around.

Although the heat was stifling and beads of sweat bubbled on her forehead, she still pulled the white bolero cardigan over her shoulder. Her skin was fair and delicate and burnt easily. Yesterday's exposure to the sun had reddened her skin which now tingled with painful little needles. She couldn't afford such a look. A Caribbean tan was what she aspired to, something that could be bought over the counter at exclusive salons. No good came of ruining an expensive fake tan even if you were very rich.

She crouched down lower behind the rocks and gathered her thoughts. She needed to keep her mind on the task in hand. Now was not the time to worry about her looks. Plenty of time for that much later, she thought with a satisfied smile.

There was that other business that needed attention as well. Zach deciding to come clean and tell all made her very nervous. Some secrets were never meant to be told. Some secrets were dangerous. A past murder was one such secret, one that could destroy the lives of them all, especially hers and Felicity's. The boys mattered least to her. Michael and James were Zach's sons from his first marriage to Wendy. They would remain relatively untouched by such a sordid scandal. Michael, because he was a hard, cold man who was gradually sinking into a pit of debt and drugs, and James because his world was open and simple.

She harboured no emotion for either of them. Felicity was her child, her flesh and blood and that was what mattered. That and several million pounds.

People had killed for less. Zach had given her no option. He had to die and die quickly. Today. She fingered the weapon tucked in the pocket of her shorts and carried on with her careful surveillance.

She watched as Ian climbed over the exposed rocks and disappeared from view. The low tide had made the hidden cove accessible. Zach was there. He would be sat in his deckchair, staring out to sea, waiting, thinking, not expecting nor welcoming an audience from anyone, including his wife. She hoped Ian would be quick. Time was precious and there was little of it left. Once in the house, her husband would shut himself away in the study. Guests would intrude and make privacy impossible. You couldn't kill a man in a busy home.

Muriel had watched her husband leave the house and walk towards the beach. Already suspicious, she had waited until he was out of sight, then followed closely behind. She knew where he was going. He was going to meet Jennifer. They were having an affair. Did they think she was so stupid that she wouldn't notice the averted eyes, the sly smiles, the not so discreet touching of hands?

She wished she cared enough to be angry, to feel something, but there was no love between them, nothing tangible, just a blatant indifference. She watched his back as he stumbled across the pebbles. Then he stopped, a black rigid figure, stark against a blue horizon, staring out to sea. She knew her husband well, especially when he was absorbed in his dark world with his dark thoughts. What did I ever see in him? she thought to herself. What kind of a devil did I tie myself to? His face materialised in her mind. Hard, cruel lines, menacing black eyes. It was all there and yet he was nothing. He had nothing. No looks, no money, no faith. Just a haunting blackness which had surrounded her life from the day they'd met. In her mind she stepped away from him, kept herself apart from his claustrophobic presence and let her eyes wander over him. It was safer this way. In real life his voice would thunder at her, his eyes would rake over her and make her cringe with a fear she couldn't identify.

From this vantage point she was strong. Her eyes travelled from the top of his head down over his body. He was a lean and fit looking man but his face was so taut his skin looked like it had been stretched like cling film over his angular skull. His mouth was hard, his eyes dark and hostile. There was nothing remotely attractive or nice about her husband. Yet, even though she was totally indifferent to him, she had to know. Were they really sleeping together? And if they were, what was she going to do about it?

When the invitation had arrived, Ian's face had turned a ghastly grey. Muriel had been quite surprised by his reaction and had taken the card from his hands but could see nothing on there that could account for such a fearful response. Yet Ian had been nervous from that moment, stricken-looking, his eyes darting unseeingly. Muriel couldn't help herself. She was so exulted inside, she relished his fear although she dared not show it. Her husband was afraid and it made her feel strong. She had to keep averting her face so her husband wouldn't see the pleasure she felt from his discomfort.

So she followed her husband and stood in the shadow of the trees. She noticed him hesitating, then, finally, as if gathering enough courage, he disappeared out of sight towards Funnel Cove. And Zach.

Muriel decided to wait. She gathered her brown cardigan over her shoulders. A blissful contentment washed over her. Had Zach summoned Ian to his cove by the sea? Was he going to confront Ian about his affair with Jennifer. Oh God, I hope so, she prayed. Of course, she did have it in her power to persuade Zach to keep quiet and protect her husband. She might just do that but not for Ian's sake. No… it would be for her sake. She had quite a lot of secrets herself that were best kept hidden.

Michael Allington stood on the cliff's edge and looked down on to the beach. From that height he could see all over the valley of Priests Finger, including the manor house and gardens. He saw old Percy Crouch high on the imposing cliff top striding towards the remains of St Magnus church that edged his farmhouse. He watched as the Reverend Peaceful, stalked silently by his strange wife, walk down to the water's edge and hover there before moving out of sight into the cove. He knelt down and peered over the edge, and watched his stepmother hiding behind the rocks. Something was going on. People were gravitating towards his father. He'd been about to do the same. Now he held back and laid down on the dry earth putting his thoughts and ideas in order.

What he had to say to his father wouldn't take long. What he had to do would be even faster. Both, however, demanded privacy.

Until a couple of weeks ago, Michael hadn't realised just how rational and sharp his father was. Since winning the lottery and becoming outrageously wealthy, the man had wallowed in his fortune. He'd acted as if he was unaware how fast his prosperity was dwindling. And it was disappearing fast.

And now, to give millions of pounds away? It didn't bear thinking about. Where would that leave them, the family? Him? Michael had debts, lots of them. Money was as essential to him as breathing and now 'dear daddy' was going to curtail their spending. What if his father found out about his gambling debts and his little drug problem? Not that he was addicted, of course. He could give them up whenever he chose to do so but now was not a good time, especially since 'dear daddy' had had his eureka moment.

He smiled to himself, a dreamy, hopeful smile. Wouldn't it be convenient if his father just happened to drop dead? Just like that. No fuss, no bother. A quick, fatal heart attack would be just the ticket. Or maybe someone else would murder him? After all, if his children didn't like him and his wife certainly didn't, then maybe others hated him enough to kill him.

So now he would wait. He took out a cigarette and lit it, drawing the nicotine deep into his lungs. It had an immediate, calming effect and he stretched out dangling his feet over the edge of the cliff. From his pocket, he drew out a weapon and placed it beside him on the grass. He looked at it. This was his safety net, his peace of mind. When he went to see his father, this would be his companion, his friend, and hopefully lead to a more prosperous future.

At this point Michael reflected, murder could be quite challenging when everybody seemed to want to visit the intended victim. He drew one long lasting drag on his cigarette and flicked it into the air. The stub landed a few feet away and smouldered in the dry grass. He leant back on his hands and gazed abstractedly up at the blue sky.

Felicity had never been so bored in all her life, or so unhappy. On arriving home she'd found the house empty and no one in sight. Having just spent several hours on the road, most of them, it seemed, on the Weymouth seafront, due to an accident on the bypass, she'd expected some kind of reception when she walked through the door. She had been away for two months and thought somebody would be at home to welcome her back. After calling out for her mother and getting an eerie nothingness in reply, she broached the back garden by means of Daddy's study.

Just great, she thought. Everyone was probably on the beach, not one of them giving her a second thought. Felicity hated coming home more and more. Freedom had proved to be seductive and homecomings were short-lived. Walking into the house and realising that no one seemed bothered about being here for her fuelled her resentment towards her family.

She stomped off the patio and strode down the garden path. Taking the old route, the one that led directly to her father's private cove, she cursed herself for not changing out of her heels and into flatter, more sensible shoes. Her heels snagged on the weeds and she stumbled, twisting her ankle. She cursed loudly. "Shit. Shit. Shit. That bloody hurt." She rubbed the sore skin, hobbling on one leg. Felicity realised there was no way she would be able to navigate the steep incline on to the beach and although it was important that she speak to Daddy, it wasn't worth breaking her neck for.

However, everyone knew not to disturb him when he sat in the cove, especially her half-brothers, but she was Daddy's little girl and perhaps a call from her would bring him hurrying up the cliff steps where they could speak together.

It would be good to talk. Things had to be said, and no matter how unpleasant the words were going to be, she and Daddy did have an understanding. He would get angry, she would cry, it would be the usual scenario. Whereas her mother would blow a fuse when she found out what Felicity had done, she was confident that Daddy wouldn't react in quite the same way.

Besides, she knew things. Things she was sure Daddy would hate people to know about. She remembered that one night, when she couldn't sleep. It had been a humid night, the beginning of another hot summer. Lying wide awake on top of the sheets, she had heard furtive sounds in the garden. She'd seen her dad sneaking across the lawn and had followed him down to the beach. Crouched down behind a rock she had watched Daddy. He'd stripped down until he was completely naked, his flaccid skin shimmering with sweat in the moonlight. What followed was something so obscene, something so disgusting it would scar her for the rest of her life. The memory still had the power to make her shudder. God. It was so gross.

Shaking away all unpleasant thoughts, she broke through the trees and on to a patch of dry mud. She was a few feet away from the edge of the cliff and the crumbling steps that staggered down to the pebbled cove when she paused and stared out to sea. Was this what Daddy meant with his party tonight? she wondered. Was he going to confess, to admit to his affair in front of all their friends?

Felicity wavered. She had no feelings towards her father, but mother said he'd been acting strange just lately. Apparently he'd had some sort of vision and now he'd gone all godly and holy. Some rubbish about giving his money away to the poor and needy and bearing his soul, or something like that. And if that wasn't enough, Julian's news had devastated her. It had been on her mind for days now, gnawing at her and making her question everything about her life. The whole bloody thing was a mess and it was all Daddy's fault. And what if the press got on to it? She shuddered. It just didn't bear thinking about.

She pulled herself together. Well that wouldn't do at all. What would her friends think? And more importantly, what would Julian say? No. There was no way out of it. She would have to speak to him. Today. Now. Oh God, she thought, if only he were dead.

Miss Mary Joyce Battersby, retired school mistress of the parish of Bridport, stood on the edge of the woods and watched the progress of James Allington. The man's lumbering gait steered him from the back of the manor, over the farm gate and across the worn path that bordered the woods. He stopped about twenty feet from her, dithering and fidgeting.

Miss Battersby couldn't stand the young man or his family. The boy, for that was how she referred to him, even though he had to be in his thirties, was simple yet exceedingly sly. She hated the way he watched everyone, sucking information like a sponge and storing it up in his tiny brain. *So like his father.*

They were a loud, brash family and had been the bane of her life since they had moved to the tiny village two years previously. She'd recognised Zach immediately. That venomous little brat from Form F. He'd made her life hell every day at school, tormenting her with the knowledge he'd gained from being nosy and a sneak. It had been blackmail then and it was blackmail now and she could stand it no longer.

The day he'd left the school had been one of her happiest, even though he had taken her secret with him. She'd believed that was the end of it. She'd thought he'd forgotten. How stupid of her. An intelligent woman, she should have known that little 'slip' would one day come back to haunt her.

Tonight though, the nightmare would be over. She was old now. Wrinkled and worn down by life. Age had shrunk her. Her tall upright frame had withered, becoming spindly and bony. Deep set wrinkles crisscrossed her face. Her pale eyes drowned in their sockets and the skin shaping her skull was as transparent as tracing paper.

She was dying. Her life was useless and irrelevant. No one would miss her. Any family she may have had were lost in the mists of time. Would she leave an impression on this life? she wondered. Mentally, she shook her head. Of course not. She was a nobody. One of life's forgotten creatures.

She rubbed her gnarled hands together. Even in the blistering heat her thin weak body had no way of combating the cold in the shade of the trees. She was on a mission, though. Here beneath the heavy laden branches was a small pod of death cap mushrooms, carefully nurtured and preserved by her for the moment she had been anticipating for some time. A night for revelations Zach had written. A night for murder, more like it, she thought.

After all, she had to do something to give credence to her time on earth and she was never one to waste an opportunity.

It would be nice to leave a memory. She could imagine it clearly. Oh yes, people would say. You remember that Miss Battersby. Wasn't she the woman who murdered that man who won all those millions?

She had conquered many adversaries in her long life. How hard could it be to get rid of just one more? Looking over her shoulder, she saw James getting closer. With a determined glint in her eyes she slipped quietly into the woods.

James didn't understand. His little world had gone crazy. Flissy had vanished in a puff of smoke one day, her car piled high with suitcases, speeding away from the house. He missed her a lot. She was the only one in the house that gave him any attention, albeit reluctantly. Mike had been acting strangely and sneaking out of the house when it was dark and everyone was supposed to be in bed. Several times James had shouted from his bedroom window and asked him where he was going, but Mike always ignored him as he disappeared into the darkness. James was afraid of the inky shadows, so he stayed awake and listened.

He had good ears and he heard things and remembered. His head was so busy with all the secrets he had collected, it was like a scrapbook in his mind.

Where did Michael go? Sometimes he saw Daddy go out as well. The door beneath his bedroom window would close with a little snap and James would sneak across his room and peer down into the garden. He saw lots of things which confused him. What did it all mean?

And what about Daddy? He'd been laughing a lot this last few weeks and saying funny things about heaven, love and a man who sat in a tree. Mummy kept shouting and screaming at him and calling him horrible names. Her high pitched screams would reverberate through his head. 'Bastard. Bastard,' were horrible words that echoed around the house. "I hate you so much," his mother had yelled so many times. "You make me sick." And Daddy would just laugh. That frightened James because he didn't like loud noises. He would shut himself away in his room and put his fingers in his ears.

Last night had been the worst ever. The door of the lounge had been slammed shut. Loud running feet on the stairs as his father ran up and his mother, screaming from

16

the hallway. James had put his fingers in in ears but it hadn't been enough to drown out the shouting. So he'd hugged himself, rocking to and fro, his head banging on the wall. He'd been naked due to the hot night but suddenly he was freezing. He'd pulled the quilt up to his neck, hoping it would protect him but it hadn't helped.

"I'll kill you before I let you give our money away," Mummy had screeched.

Daddy had shouted back, "It's my money, I tell you. It's mine and I'll do as I damn well please."

"Go to bloody hell then."

"I'm already there." And Daddy's laughter had followed him until he'd shut the door of his bedroom behind him.

Now the nightmare of the night before was back haunting James. When he woke up and dressed he could hear voices. The God man was there with his funny wife. He recognised the God man's gruff voice and his wife's whinny one. They'd been calling each other bad names just like Mummy and Daddy. Why were they in the house? he asked himself. They had their own house just up the road in Boggy Lane and the party wasn't until tonight, so they were very early.

Then, he thought he heard Flissy calling out for Mummy. That was impossible though. Flissy didn't live in the house any more. Still, he'd rushed downstairs just in case she was there but the rooms were empty, everyone had gone. Even Elsa, who worked in the kitchen wasn't around.

He stayed in the house for a little while but the emptiness made him nervous so he decided he had better go and look for someone. He knew that Daddy would be down at the cove, but James wasn't allowed down there. It was too dangerous he'd been told. He might fall down the cliffs. Sometimes though, he still liked to have a peek. He would lie down on his tummy and poke his head over the top and there he would watch Daddy.

James chose the shortcut across the farmer's field. He kept close to the trees so that the farmer wouldn't see him.

17

Many times the horrible man had shouted at him for trespassing so he crept softly along and watched all the time. When he saw Miss Battersby ahead of him he slowed down and waited until she went in the trees. He hoped she didn't see him. Miss Battersby was a nasty old lady. She called him names. She called him 'stupid boy'. James hated that. He waited until he was sure she was gone then he darted across part of the open field.

He thought he saw the farmer walking near the church graveyard so he skirted around, took cover by the old barn, and gingerly approached the cliff top. Lying down on the dry grass, he waited. Voices came to him from the cove, but they were mumbled and jumbled. It was difficult to look over the edge without being seen but he could see the boats in the water and make out the larger ships far out at sea. A helicopter flew overhead, the whirling blades slicing through the air. James ignored it. He wanted to see who else was in the cove.

Daddy was going to be angry. It was his private time. He didn't like visitors when he was sat in his deckchair. James thought he heard a strange 'pop' and a tiny cry. Seagulls maybe. Still, James thought, he would wait. Just for a little while.

Zach Allington had stumbled across Funnel Cove a couple of years previously and had immediately been taken by the big house and private beach. In an instant he'd decided he must have the manor house and when he saw the surrounding land and its potential as a building plot for exclusive homes, he went straight to the agents. With money no object he had bought a huge chunk of the Dorset countryside. The cove had been named after William Funnel who, it was reported, brought the plague into the village on his boat. Smuggling had been a lucrative business even then and evidence of that past still showed itself when heavy iron hooks, embedded into the hard rocks became exposed at low tide. Small boats were hauled on to the beach by the peasants and the hooks may even have been used when it was rumoured that the future Charles II, on a fleeting visit, landed on the beach to seek refuge in what was the old priory that had stood there before the manor was built.

Tales of treachery and disease didn't put Zach off, though. If anything, the past history of the area added to the charm of the house and tiny hamlet. The absolute perfection of the cove, the clear blue sea, the gulls swooping with their young, Zach had found his heaven. With no consultation with his wife or family, he had bought his piece of Dorset and had lorded it over the land ever since.

Now he sat in his deckchair, his hands folded in his lap and stared towards the horizon. It was August. England was still in the grip of its balmiest summer ever. The tide was out, but soon it would turn and in a few hours the cove would be underwater again. Now though, the receding tide had left behind curtains of soggy green and brown seaweed, draped over rocks, drying quickly in the blistering heat. To some, the smell of stagnant seaweed was nauseating. To Zach, it was the fresh aroma of the sea that had once teased and seduced his nostrils.

His regretful sigh made a gurgling noise in his throat. His vision was fading. He could just make out a small sail-less yacht close to the shore. It skimmed by, barely causing a ripple on the calm surface of the water. A helicopter buzzed somewhere overhead the whirling blades fading into the distance.

Out at sea, invisible to Zach, came the drone of shipping passing through the Channel and somewhere, close by, yet hidden from the secluded cove, the irritating whine of jet skis cleaving through the water. The intrusive sounds, getting louder and louder, drowned out the gentler sighs of the sea as it lapped the craggy shore.

Zach was dying. He could feel the blood mingling with his sweat, trickling down the side of his face. As quickly as it soaked into his wrinkles, the gore dried and stretched his skin. He could no longer taste the salt on his lips or feel the breeze on his skin. The blue of the sea and sky were gone forever and the smell of life? He was confused. Where was it?

He thought his heart would break. So many things to do. Vague, lost memories clamoured for attention. Jennifer, Felicity, Michael and James. A message for Evangeline. Doctors. Money. God? As he remembered each thought, so it vanished into a hazy fog and slipped away, to be swallowed by eternity.

In that last moment, suspended between life and death, he felt souls surrounding him. He heard their mournful cries, hands touching him, faces and whispers by his ears. What were they saying? Voices so far away.

His lips moved. His breath hammered in his brain. He heard his own voice, loud and clear, echoing in his head. He thought he knew who had killed him. A vague shadow out of the corner of his eye, a flash of light. But he didn't understand. His last emotion, his last sense. His last conscious thought. Why would anyone want him dead?

Chapter Two

The tide was creeping up the shore, gathering speed as the wind began to pick up pace. Rocks and seaweed were no longer exposed to the sun, the cove was once again inaccessible from the beach. Like King Canute facing a stand-off against the sea, the body of the deceased remained in the deckchair, the eyes blank and unseeing.

DS Bill South cursed under his breath and shook his soggy foot. "We need to move the body, sir," he said to the man at his side. "At the rate the tide's coming in, we'll be under water in a short while."

His superior, DCI Andrew Fortune, had his head bent over the corpse. He was examining the small cavity left by the bullet where it had entered the temple from the victim's right. "No exit wound," he muttered to himself, ignoring his sergeant's concerns. "At least we don't have to search for the bullet."

He remained stooped and circled the dead body. He saw a man, in his late fifties, early sixties. Grey hair was spread thinly over a large skull, the skin on the face was pitted and weather worn. Layers of blood streaked down towards a relaxed mouth, where a pale tongue protruded between nicotine stained teeth. Long flaccid jowls hung down and rested on hunched shoulders.

Zach Allington had been out in the sun for several hours and dead for at least two of them. Already the chemical process of decomposition had begun. The blood was sinking, and the skin paling. Only the dead man's stomach, a large rotund ball of sun-burnt flesh, gave a sense of a once human being.

It always amazed Andy how newly dead bodies shrank and folded in on themselves as if, once the soul had departed, the insides just disintegrated. Decay was a dreadful thing, he thought.

He was released from his introspection by his DS. "They've found the weapon, sir. It was dumped behind the rocks. A nice little shooter."

Andy Fortune straightened up and slowly creaked his back and neck into place. He looked around, noting the SOCOs milling around. They were nearly finished. Kennet, the photographer was slowly climbing the jagged steps to the top of the cliffs. Other officers were packing up, bagging objects collected from the scene of the crime, butt ends and wrappers included. Nothing would be overlooked, his team was thorough.

He gave the bagging men a discreet nod. The late Mr Allington needed to be moved. In another few hours they would all be standing in three foot of seawater. Gathering evidence took time but everything on this case, if it wasn't bagged quickly, would be destroyed by the incoming tide.

He stepped away from the deckchair and allowed his men to do their jobs. The CID unit had been dispatched from nearby Abbotswood where they'd just been assigned. DS South and he had transferred from inner London on a temporary basis and this was only their second murder in Dorset.

As the Senior Investigation Officer he needed to assert his authority as quickly as possible. He knew his team were good, he'd been watching closely for the past few weeks. He anticipated that this could be the case that gelled the team together.

"This is better, sir. A good old fashioned shooting," Bill South said with relish. "After reading old reports of past crimes in this area it's refreshing to get back to basics. That last homicide involving Mr Bradley, in the garden, wearing Marigolds and a clementine stuffed in his mouth fair turned my stomach." He shuddered dramatically. "After that, this should be nice and straight forward."

"I know what you mean, South, but I don't think it's that cut and dried." He looked at the man who had been his sidekick for the last two years. Bill South was a large, stocky true Londoner. Bald as a coot and hard as nails. Big as he was though, he could run like a whippet. Many a criminal had been surprised at the agility of the heavy-set man especially when they were bowled over mid stride.

A natty dresser though and a godsend in the office. Bill was a dab hand on the computer, he kept meticulous records, and when it came to gathering information and writing reports, he was your man.

He was speaking again. "What about our audience, sir?" he asked, indicating with a nod of his head to the small crowd gathered at the top of the cliff. "His missus is up there and the rest of family including house guests. We tried to move them to the house but they insisted on staying until the deceased has been moved."

Andy Fortune looked over his shoulder. A small procession was making its way up the side of the cliff, the dead man now in a black bag being gently manoeuvred. The progress was slow and cumbersome as it was quite a steep climb. Above them the observers watched. He couldn't see much emotion on their faces and there certainly seemed to be no tears but he knew that type of observation was useless. People reacted to death in many different ways, yet he was pretty sure that at least one of them was a murderer.

A stranger would hardly visit a secluded cove on the Dorset coast and blow the brains out of a lonely occupant sitting minding his own business.

A splash of cold water soaking his shoes and hem of his trousers brought him out of his reverie. Time was moving on. He checked his watch. Just after three. The afternoon was pushing towards a close. "Right, South. Let's get out of here," he said. "We need to get back to the manor and get the interviews under way."

They both clambered up the slate grey face of the cliff. Andy reached for the outstretched hand and grabbed it for the final step on to the grassy verge. It was Squires, the coroner. They'd only met once so Andy continued contact and shook the man's hand. The nod of his head was deferential. "DCI Fortune, Mr Squires, and this is DS South." He introduced the man rubbing the knees of his suit. "We met last week if you remember?"

Squires and South nodded to each other. "I remember you both, Detective Chief Inspector. Perhaps you'd better call me Mark," he suggested.

"Of course, Mark. If I can just speak to my DS then I'll have a word with you." He turned to South. "Get all the witnesses up to the house and sort out an interview room. I'll follow you in a while. We need to get preliminary statements started. I want to know everyone's movements since breakfast, and get me a general layout of the house and area, and which people live in the vicinity of the dead man's residence. Get as many officers as you can on to it and I'll be with you shortly." DS South nodded and walked towards the observers who were now being ushered away from the scene by a determined uniformed officer.

Andy turned to the man waiting patiently. "Right, Mark, let's get on. What can you tell me at this point?" he asked the coroner. Mark Squires was a short wiry man with greasy hair but he had an intelligent face and clear honest eyes. He was probably in his early forties and seemed more approachable than Andy was used to. Banks and Shaw, the coroners adjoined to his London station, made life difficult and obtaining information was a long drawn out process.

Mark squinted against the sun, turned and started walking towards the ruins of the church. The breeze, slight as it was, was welcome on the men's backs. Both men carried their jackets over their arms.

Mark began. He had a soft Dorset accent. "White male, sixty-one years of age. Approximately five foot eleven. Death occurred about twelve forty-five" He held his hand up when Andy went to interrupt. "I know that because our victim didn't die instantly. Apparently he said a few words before he departed this life."

He stopped and so did Andy. They both looked back towards the cove. "The victim was facing the sea, so our murderer must have approached from behind and on the victim's right. He fired, and the bullet entered at the location of the temporal lobe in the first instance. The general trajectory might mean the bullet is lodged behind our victim's left eye. That's all I can say for the moment until I get him on the slab." He held out his hand. "My car's parked at the farm so I'll bid you goodbye. Give me two days and I should have the ballistic results and all other general information." And with that he strode off leaving Andy to make his way slowly to the house.

Priest Finger manor had prime position at the bottom of the village. With only one access from the B3157 and down a long, narrow one lane track, the house perched itself precariously on a rocky mound. The lawns surrounding the house sloped down towards a strip of silver maple trees that surrounded the property, and at the back of the building, a well-worn path broke through the trees to the shingled beach.

All cars were parked at the front of the house. From there, the wide gravelled path meandered around the main body of the house and opened up on to a square of land at the rear, an area that mirrored the front. Here a columned concrete portal, with wide wooden doors at the top of centuries old curved steps, centred the facade of the building.

DCI Fortune stood on the dry, patchy lawn and faced the manor. Legend had it that some time during late September 1651, en route to Charmouth, the then King Charles II was betrayed as he left the village. The local priest had pointed his finger at the priory, which had stood in place of the manor all those centuries ago, causing Captain Macey's troops to follow in hot pursuit. They'd nearly caught King Charles, and it was only by hiding in Badgers Wood that the king and his supporters evaded capture.

The manor, a square, Georgian style building built in the late 1700s stood solid but weather beaten. Blasted by years of sea spray its frontage had a battered uncared for look, its concrete lintels and sills were clipped and crumbling, the cladding broken away in several places. Salt was a relentless predator and could erode the sturdiness of most buildings. On the whole though, the house had a certain charm. The present owners had obviously made an effort to improve the appearance of the building, a lot of the rendering had been repaired and several licks of paint had been applied.

A modern glass conservatory fronted the left side of the house whilst on the right of the door and cornering the house was a wide concrete patio surrounded by a foot high ornate balustrade.

Andy walked up the steps. A uniformed officer stood guard and moved aside as his senior approached. He pushed open the heavy door and entered a large hallway. Huge oak panels covered the walls and a heavy chandelier hung from the high ceiling. A couple of high backed chairs were placed in each corner and a small curved table sat beside the staircase with a bowl of fresh flowers on it. A cream coloured rug gave relief to the dark flagstones. It was certainly much cooler within the thick walls and he took a few moments to adjust to the welcome coolness.

"In here, sir," DS Stone called from one of four doorways.

The room he entered was large and similar in decor to the hallway. Heavy wooded panelling dominated one wall while the other walls were painted a dull, sage green. Fortunately, the large French windows, which led on to the garden via the patio, let in lots of light, whilst heavy glass doors, wedged open by grotesque concrete statues let in the very slightest of scented sea air. Cream-coloured transparent voiles gently swayed.

Against the panelled wall was a long glass cabinet. Lit up by a solitary light it drew attention to a wide variety of small firearms. Andy gave it a cursory glance. Plenty of time for that later, he thought. He let his eyes wander around the rest of the room. On one of the walls, the one behind the door and facing the garden, were four paintings. They depicted man and horse, and man and dog in various poses. He wasn't an art lover but he thought they looked expensive.

It was obviously the late Mr Allington's study. Objects of his past presence were evident on the big mahogany desk which faced the cabinet. Cigars, letters, a big onyx ashtray and a black laptop sat tidily in their allotted places.

On either side of the desk were two expensive leather backed chairs. The one facing the wall was occupied. He took the other chair, eased himself back and observed the man opposite. "And this is?" he asked his Detective Sergeant.

South moved forward and hovered over the desk. He opened up a small, black notebook. "James Allington, sir. Youngest son of the deceased. He was the last person to see the deceased alive and heard his final words."

Andy Fortune sat up straighter in his chair. Resting his elbows on the table and folding his hands beneath his chin, he was instantly alert. Looking with more interest at the man before him, Andy noted the young man's nervousness. James Allington shifted restlessly, his eyes darted from side to side, deliberately avoiding the two detectives. This was a man who had other underlying problems, DCI Fortune thought. He stared hard at the man willing him to meet his eyes.

Gently, gently with this one he decided. "Mr Allington," he began coaxingly. "I'm sorry to have to ask you questions at such a difficult time, but we need to know who killed your father, and we believe you were the last person to see your father alive." He waited for a reaction. Nothing. The hands in the man's lap remained clenched, the eyes remained downcast. "Mr Allington," he urged, "Can you tell us what your father said please?"

James's head jerked up with a snap. "Is he dead now? He looked dead. I called his name. There was blood on his face." The sentences were stilted. The voice was questioning and simple. Now the men's eyes met. One pair bewildered the other watchful.

Leaning farther over the desk he asked again, "What did he say, James? Can you remember?" he coaxed. It was like questioning a child.

James looked earnest. "I don't know what he meant," he said, his eyes wild. "I didn't understand. Did he die?" he asked innocently.

Andy pressed on regardless. "What did he say, James? It's very important that you remember."

"He was calling. He said it was his call." James slapped his hands on his thighs. "He found God, you know. He heard voices he did. Ask Mummy. Mummy shouted at him all the time. Mummy was angry. Do you want to know what I do when Mummy shouts?"

Andy's brown eyes met South's. His DS was scribbling in the notebook taking in every word. Andy raised his eyebrows, South shrugged. "Okay, James. What do you do?" he asked patiently.

James shook with excitement and wrapped his arms around himself. "I put my fingers in my ears." He laughed as if he'd said something truly amazing.

DCI Fortune was resigned. An on the spot witness and totally unreliable. The most useless of testimonies. He looked at the man who was staring back at him so hopefully. He saw a man in his middle thirties with fair hair and a long face. He bore a striking facial resemblance to his father but was of a much slimmer build. In fact James Allington wore a malnourished look that wouldn't look out of place in one of those old fashioned workhouses of the Victorian era. Andy shook his head. "What a waste," he said under his breath. "South?" Andy's voice was quiet. "Take Mr Allington out and hand him over to a member of the family then come straight back. Get Barton to gather up the suspects and put them somewhere comfortable. No one must leave the house until I say so. Also, check to see if the preliminary statements are ready. We'd better have a chat before we do any more interviews."

South went out closing the door softly behind him. Andy could hear muted voices in the hallway. He stood up and walked round the table to the cabinet. Inside the glass case lay three rows of small guns. He had limited knowledge of firearms but he thought they were all lady guns and that some were most in Europe.

On the right of the top shelf was an empty space. The light sheen of dust marked out the shape of another tiny hand gun. He hoped it was the one found at the scene of the murder. Valuable time could be saved if it were. He noted that one of the glass doors was slightly open. There was also a little brass key in the lock. Tilting his head one way and then the other, he looked for fingerprints, but the glass was clear. He would get the cabinet dusted as quickly as he could, but he wasn't hopeful of a find. Criminals were aware of forensic science nowadays and knew all the tricks to avoid detection.

South slipped into the room with another member of the team and stood beside him. "I've brought Constable Collins to see you, sir. I thought he might be able to help. He recognised the gun we found."

Collins puffed out his chest. He'd been pooling his knowledge of guns for some time now, waiting for this very moment. His voice was proud. "It's a Lady Darringer, sir. American. Nice and easy to load and shoot. Mainly sold to women because it's so compact and fits easily into their handbags. A pretty accessory and easy to conceal."

Not having seen the weapon the DCI asked, "How big is it? What's its capabilities?"

"The barrel's about three inches and the overall length is four and half inches, sir. With a 32 magnum calibre. This one's a pretty elaborate model. Expensive ivory grips, inlaid with gold. A collector's item, highly sort after. I imagine this is a bespoke gun."

"And obviously lethal," South observed.

"Not necessarily, sir. These guns generally have what they call in America, reasonable stopping power. I'd say our murderer was either an expert shot, or plain lucky."

"What distance was it fired from?" Andy asked.

His sergeant made a little moue with his lips. "Twelve feet max, sir. Any farther back and the outcome could have been a lot different."

DS South pointed to the other guns in the cabinet. "Did our murderer pick the best gun? These others look impressive."

Collins scanned with his expert eyes. "Quite a few Berettas," he said. He pointed some out. "That's a Beretta M418. Italian. Lovely pocket pistol," he said enviously. "And that semi-automatic?" he marked out another one. "A BU9 Nato. Actually has six rounds in a single column box magazine. This is a good healthy collection." He looked at his superior. "If these guns are all loaded, then I reckon the murderer picked the first one to hand and got lucky."

"Well thank you, Collins, for your observations. Get back out there with our suspects and when you get five minutes, try and arrange for some tea and perhaps some sandwiches. Make sure everyone has something to eat then we'll proceed with the interviews in half an hour or so." As the officer turned to leave he added, "You'd better warn the family and guests that it could take some time to get this done and dusted. Round up the guests first so that they can leave if the interviews are satisfactory."

His Sergeant took his leave. South turned to his boss. They walked over to the French doors. "What do you think of our Mr James then, sir?"

DCI Fortune sighed. He was not happy. "Not really reliable is he? I think there may be medical difficulties with that one. Quite possibly Asperger's. He seems adamant though. The deceased said it was his call or his calling." He shook his head and chewed on his lip. "His call to do what, South?"

"Haven't a clue, sir." A knock at the door interrupted them. They walked back into the room. South opened the door and stood back. A woman entered, possibly in her early thirties in their estimation. She crossed to the desk bearing a tray of assorted sandwiches and enough tea for them both.

"Ta love," South said appreciatively. "I'm starving." He grabbed a sandwich and took a large bite. "Now, before you go. What's your name and what are you in this here household?" He gave the woman a wide lecherous grin. It was the sort of grin that got women and men into trouble. The DCI shook his head. How South got away with it in these modern times of equality constantly amazed his superior officer.

DCI Fortune smiled wryly, sat back and watched South interrogate the woman. She wasn't particularly attractive but she did have nice bright eyes and well-defined bone structure. Her hair, although an effervescent bubble gum pink and rolled up in a French pleat, suited her.

Being in the presence of police officers didn't intimidate her either. She faced DS South squarely.

"My names Elsa, sir. I help out in the kitchen and do general house-keeping. Nothing fancy though. I work Tuesday through to Saturday and have Sunday and Monday off."

"How did you get on with Mr Allington, the deceased, Elsa?" South asked as he pulled out the chair and invited her to sit down. He took out his notebook.

Elsa shrugged. "He was alright, sir. A bit of a grump and very particular about things. He paid well and didn't give me any grief. As long as I did my job and didn't bother him then he was okay. But I will say this, sir," she leant forward and lowered her voice to a soft whisper, "he had a bit of a temper when it came to the family, but just lately he's been real sweet like." She looked over her shoulder towards the door. "You see, he'd had an amifany a couple of weeks ago and went all peculiar." Her pink head nodded sagely.

DCI Fortune stretched out his arms on the desk and clasped his hands together. "I think you mean an epiphany, Elsa," he corrected. "What happened exactly and can you remember when it occurred?"

She scrunched up her face. "I don't rightly know because it happened on my day off. So that would have been Sunday. Yes, that's right. Sunday was my birthday so I think it might have been Saturday night when he woke up and had his epiphany."

South counted the days off his fingers. "That will be two weeks today then," he calculated. "Did he have a vision or a dream? What was this epiphany all about?"

"Well, sir. I don't rightly know if he saw anything but I heard he was going to give all his money away," she confided. "And I think the party tonight was to tell everyone. He had a few secrets to tell as well. I know the family weren't happy about it. There's been some fierce arguing lately. Mrs Allington's been screaming her head off, telling her husband that he's mad and a few choice words on top of that. She was so angry she didn't care who heard her."

Well, well, thought DCI Fortune. A strong motive to kill a man. Money and secrets all packaged into one space. It was highly probable that any invited guest would also be subjected to some sort of exposure. Interesting, he thought.

Allowing his DS to carry on questioning the woman he walked back over to the open patio doors. Before he stepped outside on to the patio he looked back over his shoulder.

"Who opened these doors, Elsa?" he asked.

"I did, sir," she admitted. "When I arrive at work at seven o'clock, that's one of the first things I do. Mr Allington likes… I mean liked to have the room aired before he came in after breakfast. He smoked those big cigars and this room always smelt bad."

"What time did you leave the house today?"

"About eleven thirty I think. I had to get some provisions in for the party tonight. I got back about half past one."

"So anyone could have wandered into this room from the garden or the hallway without being observed?"

"Oh yes, sir." She nodded her head in agreement. "All the family use this room as a shortcut on to the patio and gardens, and the beach as well. The only time they use the lounge doors is when Mr Allington is… was in this study."

"Have you cleaned in here today, Elsa? Dusted or polished maybe?"

"Yes, I did that before I left. Mr Allington always went

down to the cove about eleven if the tide was out and that would give me time to get this room cleaned, and get the rest of downstairs cleaned. He hated the sound of the hoover."

"Thank you, Elsa. We may need to speak to you later and DS South will arrange for a statement for you to sign."

"Thank you, sir," she said and left the room giving a flirty smile to South.

Andy stepped outside on to the paved patio. This side of the house was now in the shade but the heat was still intense. South followed him. "I don't think we're going to get any clear fingerprints from that cabinet if she's cleaned in here," Andy mused. "But you can see that it was easy for our murderer to help him or herself to the weapon. It would take seconds to slip in here from the garden or house, unlock the cabinet, and back out the same way." He sighed deeply. "You'd better get Barton in here so we can go over the statements."

Barton stepped into the room. He was another bulky looking officer with broad shoulders and a thick fleshy neck. He had an intelligent face, honest eyes and a wide smile. "I've got six statements, sir, from Mrs Jennifer Allington, Mr Michael Allington, Miss Felicity Allington, the Reverend Ian Peaceful and his wife Muriel. The statement from Mr James Allington isn't very clear unfortunately." He placed them on the desk. "I've sent Collins and Townsend to collect statements from a Miss Mary Battersby who was in the vicinity and a farmer named Percy Crouch who was seen on the cliff top at the relevant time. He owns most of the land in these parts."

"Right, Barton. That's excellent." Andy sat at the desk. "You've been working this area for some years now. What's the gossip about our corpse?"

Barton took out his notebook, licked his finger and flicked over the first page. "Zacchaeus Allington, sir, also known as Zach. Born 3rd November 1952. He went to school in Hammersmith and left when he was fifteen to enter the building trade. He was the only son of a labourer and his mother was a cleaner." He flicked the page. "In 1974 at the age of twenty-two he went into partnership with Clive Traversy. He married Wendy Ridges in '75 and they had two boys, James and Michael who are aged thirty-five and thirty-seven respectively." Sergeant Barton wet his lips and carried on. "His wife died in a hit and run in '84 and he married again in 1987 to Miss Jennifer Golding. Incidentally, sir, she'd been his secretary since he began his business. Their daughter Felicity was born a year later. The business partnership ended two years ago when his partner Clive fell over the cliffs at Ringstead.

"Fell off the cliff, Sergeant?" DCI Fortune queried. "Any suspicious circumstances?"

"There were rumours of a rift, sir, but the alibis for the time in question were checked and Mrs Traversy, who stood most to gain from his death and of course Mr and Mrs Allington, all alibied each other. They were dining together at the time. Apparently Mr Traversy left the house during the party and threw himself off the cliff."

"Just like that eh?" said South, sceptically.

"Carry on, Barton," Andy interrupted.

"Well, sir. About three or four weeks after that, Mr Allington, the deceased, won seventeen million pounds on the lottery. It was a rollover and he was the only winner."

"Very fortuitous," observed Andy. "And what's been happening recently? What has our corpse done that was so bad for someone to put a hole in the side of his head?"

"From what I can gather, sir, the deceased had had a dream. Something to do with Zacchaeus the tax collector. The one from the Bible."

DS South sighed dramatically. "And what tax collector is that, Sergeant? I thought we had a nice simple murder here and what happens? We've got a dead man who converses with God." He shook his head in dismay. "Give me the gangsters in London any day. They know how to kill a man proper like."

Barton skewed him a look. "Luke 17, sir. Zacchaeus, the

tax collector, climbed a sycamore tree to get a better view of Jesus. Jesus saw him up the tree and they went to the house together where Zacchaeus promised to give half his money away."

South snorted. "Bloody ridiculous. What person in his right mind hands over millions of pounds?" he asked. Nobody answered.

DCI Fortune looked at his watch. It was now four thirty-five. Nearly three hours had passed since they'd arrived in Priest's Finger. He stood up and began pacing the room.

"Right, the conclusion is this. Our victim had some sort of a vision, and decided to give half his wealth away. Two weeks to the day he throws a party. A 'revelation party' he calls it. He gathers certain people together along with his family. Presumably, had the party gone according to plan, we can safely predict that he was going to say things that may have a detrimental effect on some of the people in this house. Therefore," he added dramatically, "Zack Allington had to die."

South nodded his head. "I agree, sir. Some of them present would be very upset about the money." He turned to Barton. "Any idea how much money we're talking about?"

"No, sir. We haven't got round to solicitors just yet. I'll get someone on to it straight away but there may be a delay 'cause it's Sunday tomorrow."

"Do your best, Sergeant. Now go and see if Collins and Townsend are back with those final statements."

As Barton opened the door they heard voices in the hallway. Andy and South looked at each other.

"I recognise that voice," South said.

"So do I," Andy said resignedly. He walked into the hallway. Two people were stood on the threshold. A police officer was blocking their way.

South was smiling. "It's alright, officer. Let them in." He reached over and shook the newcomer's hand. "Hello, Adam. How are you?" he said cheerfully.

"Hello Bill. Good to see you." The handshake was hearty.

Then he looked towards the other man.

"Hello, Andrew," he said quietly. "Good to see you too."

Andy smiled wryly and shook his head in disbelief. "Hello, Dad."

Chapter Three

Three men sat around the desk. The woman, who had arrived at the same time as Adam, had been escorted to the main lounge where everyone had congregated.

"Well, Dad. What are you doing here and who's the lovely woman?" Andy asked. He stretched his arms above his head. It had been a long day and there were many hours to go.

"I met the lady, her name's Eve Traversy by the way," he explained, "on the Cobb at Lyme Regis. We were the only two passengers on one of those charter boats that take you out along the Jurassic coast. She just happened to mention that she was on her way to Priest's Finger and I offered her a lift."

South referred to his notes. "I've heard that name. Yes. Here it is. Wife of the partner of the deceased, sir. The one that threw himself off the cliffs."

Andy ignored his DS's observation and addressed his father. "It's a bit out of your way, Dad. I thought you were staying at Bishop's Caundle?"

Adam Fortune nodded affirmation. "I was, but you remember my friend Sergeant Long?" His son nodded. "He had a bit of an accident three days ago. Done his back in. He's in hospital in Dorchester on traction, so I'm looking after the house and animals for him until they let him out. He's got one of those small cottages as you come down the lane and I've visited quite a few times." He leant over the desk with an eager look in his eyes. "So what going on, Andy? Who's the victim?"

DCI Fortune held his tongue. Instead he asked, "You know Zach Allington then?"

"So Zach's dead," Adam surmised. "Well I can't say I'm surprised. The man was a rotter through and through. I've met him quite a few times since the family moved here and I wasn't impressed. He was a bully and a cheat." He held up his hand. "I'm not saying he deserved to die mind you but he is, or more precisely was, the perfect victim."

His son smiled to himself. Since his father had been medically retired from the force he had lost a large part of himself. The gun wound that had ended his career had also destroyed his dad's life. He'd lost all his vitality and zest for living.

Now though, the sparkle was back in his eyes and a few of those deep lines on his face had magically disappeared. The puzzle of a murder was lifting his spirit.

"What about the rest of the family, Dad?" he asked encouragingly. "What can you tell me about them?"

Ex-Sergeant Fortune sat back in the chair. "The family's probably the most dysfunctional group of people I've ever met. Zach acted way above his station. He assumed that money would buy a position in higher society. He thought money could buy him whatever he wanted."

"And his wife and kids?" South asked.

"To put it short and sweet," began Adam. "Jenny Allington. Greedy and manipulative. Mike, eldest son. Again greedy and quite possibly a drug addict. James. A bit simple but very deceitful and he has a way of finding things out. That man has eyes everywhere. Felicity. A selfish girl. Thoroughly spoilt by both parents. Secretive as well. This lot hide their troubles behind a facade of family togetherness."

"Okay, Dad. Thanks for those insights." He addressed DI South, "We'd better start on the interviews now before it gets too late. Get Barton to show in the Reverend Peaceful first."

South left the room. "I suppose you want to stay in on this, Dad?" Andy guessed. He received an eager nod. "Right, go and sit by that cabinet and let us have your observations after each interview. Oh and by the way, Dad. It's good to see you."

The Reverend Ian Peaceful strode arrogantly into the room. South slipped silently and unobserved behind him. Without an invitation he sat in the chair. He did not offer his hand to be shaken nor did he engage in polite conversation, in fact he remained completely quiet and affected no words of introduction.

DCI Fortune was not intimidated by the silence. He stared hard at the man. He saw a tall lean man with angular features, slick black hair and round, black piercing eyes. It wasn't a pleasant face, the countenance was hard and unyielding. The hands, resting on black jeans were long and thin, the nails groomed. The Reverend fisted his hands and the sound of cracked knuckles splintered the silence.

DCI Fortune shuffled the papers in his hands. He read from the top statement. "I see that you are the Reverend Ian Michael Peaceful. You are sixty-two years old and you live in the village. How long have you lived here, sir?"

"Three years, Chief Inspector," he answered sharply.

"And you've been acquainted with the deceased for the last two years at least?"

"No," he denied. "Actually I've known Zach for forty-eight years. We were at school together. I was one year ahead of him. After school we lost touch, like you do." He shrugged. "We met again when Zach bought Priest's Finger Manor."

"What were your feelings towards Mr Allington? Did you know him well?"

Ian Peaceful laughed harshly. "I should say so. Zach was a wicked, evil man. Even at twelve he had a warped sense of humour. It doesn't surprise me that someone has murdered him."

"When did you last see the deceased, sir?" Andy asked.

For the first time since the interview had begun, the Reverend looked uncomfortable. He took a deep breath. "Well, I admit to seeing Zach about quarter past twelve. We had a short conversation and then I left. He was still alive and well at that time," he insisted.

"I see. And what did this conversation consist of?"

Ian Peaceful gave him an imperious look. Andy was reminded of an eagle staring haughtily from the branches of a tree or even a vicar staring down from the pulpit. "I can assure you any conversation was private and bears no relevance to the man's demise."

Andy grimaced. "This is a murder investigation, sir," he emphasized. "Anything that was said to the deceased may or may not be relevant but at this moment in time, please allow us to decide whether what you have to say is important."

Ian Peaceful took his time. He crossed his legs and plucked at an invisible speck on his trousers. His long, talon-like fingers drew the eyes of the other two occupants of the room. DCI Fortune waited.

Eventually the Reverend spoke but he kept his eyes lowered but not before he speared Andy a fierce resentful glance. With deliberate reluctance he said, "Zach was holding a party tonight. A 'revelation party' would you believe. He'd invited a few neighbours, the family and a couple of close family friends. My wife and I obviously included."

Andy referred to his notes. "Your wife is called Muriel I see. And which category do you both fit into? Friends, neighbours or both?"

The other man humphed deep in his throat. "Certainly not a friend. My wife and I moved here three years ago. We had a quiet, if reserved lifestyle. I had my writing, and my wife," he shrugged, "she did whatever women do. And then Zach appeared. Loaded with money," he sneered and shook his head. "Where's the justice, when a man like him wins millions of pounds? It's a travesty." He paused for a while and then as if talking to himself carried on, "It didn't make him happy though, did it? Tormenting everyone with his wealth and his knowledge and then he decides he wants to give it all away to charity because he's had some sort of godly vision. Pah. Ridiculous. Found God indeed."

"Not very charitable thoughts for a man of the cloth," Andy remarked.

"Hah. Charity begins at home. That's what I say. What about his wife and family? Yes, make a donation by all means, but half his millions? The man's an ass, Chief Inspector."

"Was," DC South said from the back of the room.

Ian shrugged indifferently and Andy spared a glance to his father and Bill. The former was sitting against the wall by the gun cabinet and the latter was busy writing in his notebook. "Have you been in this room before?" Andy asked carrying on with the questioning.

"Many times."

"And do you recognize the gun cabinet?"

Ian gave it a cursory glance then looked back across the table. "Of course, Chief Inspector. Zach enjoys… enjoyed collecting small firearms. He has several collections scattered around the house, but the ones in that particular cabinet are his more expensive ones. Some of them are quite rare."

"Have you handled any of them, especially recently?"

The Reverend had visibly relaxed with this new line of questioning and became quite amiable. He pondered thoughtfully. "Not recently no, but certainly around about May some time. I seem to remember being in here when he received a packet containing a couple of pieces."

"I see," Andy replied. He sat up straighter in his chair. "Right. Now to get back to our previous conversation. What did you and the late Mr Allington have a chat about this morning?"

The quick turn of questioning had the Reverend tensing again. He wasn't quick enough to hide the angry glitter in his eyes. "Detective Chief Inspector, I reiterate that this is… was," he corrected irritably, "a private matter between me and the deceased but," he held up his hand as Andy went to interrupt, "I do understand that you need to know." He took a deep breath. "As it happens, when I entered the cove, Zach was fast asleep and I was loathe to wake him. I was going to ask him to think again about the money but I lost my nerve, if you must know."

"Really," Andy said sceptically. "You're sure he was asleep and not dying with a hole in his head?" he asked brutally.

The beady eyes flicked up dangerously. "He was asleep," he said bluntly.

Andy let it go and shuffled the papers on the desk. "How

did you approach the cove?" he asked, again changing the direction of questioning. He perused a rough sketch of the cove and beach. The semi-circle of the beach was flanked either side by tall grey cliffs, the manor house providing a split between them, whilst the cove was completely surrounded. Its accessibility marked on the paper with red arrows.

"Direct from the house. I crossed the garden at about twelve, followed the pathway through the trees on to the beach. The tide was out, so I was able to make my way around the edge of the cliffs into the cove."

"You can't access the cove at high tide then?" Andy asked.

"Well I expect you could swim round, but the water rises well over a metre, and at high tide the cove is completely submerged."

"So, you walked round the bottom of the cliffs and found Mr Allington asleep in his deckchair?"

"Exactly, Chief Inspector."

"And how did you leave? The same way?"

"No, I climbed out using the steps at the rear of the cove."

Andy frowned. "You must be fit, Reverend. It's quite steep. I'm younger that you and I found it a bit of a challenge."

"It's easy when you've done it as many times as I have. You have to remember that before Zach came here and bought sole rights to the beach and cove, myself and several of the neighbours used to spend a lot of time down there."

"Did you see anyone?" Andy asked without much hope.

Nicotine stained teeth gnawed at the fat lower lip. "I did think that I heard something in the bushes when I reached the top. It was just an impression though. Some twigs snapping. Could have been James I suppose," he mused. "That man is always snooping about. He's just like his father. I wouldn't believe anything he has to say." He shrugged and averted his eyes. "I may have been mistaken though. Might have been an animal. A sheep maybe. They wander about all over the place."

"You heard no other sounds? Voices for instance?"

"Nothing."

The three experienced men in the room knew he was lying. He was holding something back. DCI Fortune was tempted to press him further but decided to try another tactic.

"The late Mr Allington sent out invitations to certain people to attend a revelation party." Ian nodded warily. "Aside from the family he'd invited you, Reverend, your wife Muriel, one Evangeline Traversy and her son Julian, a Miss Battersby and Percy Crouch and his son Ben. Why," he mused, "did he invite outsiders as it were, to reveal that he was giving away a great sum of money? That doesn't sound to plausible does it? Why have a party at all when, from what I can gather, everyone concerned already knew his intentions? It was hardly going to be a surprise was it?"

"If you knew Zach as well as I do, you wouldn't be surprised. The man was hoping for a knighthood. Having millions of pounds in the bank was never enough for him. No doubt a member of the press would have been sniffing around to report his good deed. It had nothing to do with charity I can assure you"

Andy picked up his pen and twiddled it between his finger. His brow creased in concentration. "So why call it a revelation party?" he repeated. He shook his head. "No, Reverend Peaceful, that won't wash. We believe that Mr Allington was going to expose a few secrets tonight and that was why he was murdered. Someone most certainly wanted him dead before he could say anything." His hands cuffed under his chin, elbows on the desk. "Have you a secret, sir? One that was worth murdering for?" he asked bluntly.

The talon-like fingers clenched. "Nothing that would interest you, Inspector. We all have secrets and mine are private. I refuse to volunteer any information about myself, I didn't kill the man and that's the end of it. May I go now? I must minister to Mrs Allington. The poor woman has had a dreadful shock as you can imagine." He stood up, rolling his shoulders in a military fashion.

Andy nodded curtly to South and the latter prised himself from the wall and opened the door. The Reverend left without a backward glance. South peeked out into the hall then closed the door.

"Cor blimey, sir. All fire and brimstone that one. I bet his congregation shake in their seats when he gets going."

"Umm. Did you get that all down, South? And are you okay, Dad?"

Adam Fortune nodded, stood up and walked to the desk. He was still a handsome man. Age had matured him kindly and it was difficult to imagine the pain he was constantly in. He walked with a small limp and his shoulders were slightly folded forward to compensate for the pain but he still stood shoulder to shoulder with his son. Unlike Andy's hair, which was crisp and black (inherited from his mother), Adam's was cloudy grey with flecks of freckle coloured strands. Both had olive green eyes and classic strong noses and whilst Andy's mouth was grim and straight his father's was more fleshy and full coloured. They were alike in many ways but their passion for justice was the one trait that bound them together. Good or bad, men, women or children, they worked tirelessly to get retribution for their victims. And now, for the first time it looked like they would be working together.

DCI Fortune was more than happy with this outcome. His father had a knack for drawing people out. They opened up to him and that was partly why his father had retained his sergeant rank rather than going for promotion. He was noted for being the man on the ground, following his nose, getting into people's minds. He was known as the bloodhound. When he was on the scent he never let go.

"What's your take on this, Dad?" Andy asked respectfully.

"Bit early to say, but that Reverend…" he grimaced. "Is he really a reverend I wonder?" At an affirmative nod he exclaimed, "Blimey, he's harsh. Only met him a couple of times and then I called him Mr Peaceful. He's a bit sweet on the lady of the house, so I've heard."

Andy laughed. "Didn't take you long to find that out."

His father tapped his nose. "You know me, son," he chuckled.

Leaning over the desk. Andy showed them the rough sketch of the lay of the land. They saw two half-moon shapes of the beach and the cove with a cross to mark the position of the deceased. Arrows marked the access points to the cove and several red crosses marked the position of the suspects. At the top of the paper, crosses indicated the spots where Miss Battersby, James and Percy Crouch were at about twelve o clock. Felicity and Muriel stated that they were near the house going in different directions, one towards the cove the other behind the Reverend towards the beach. Michael Allington and the deceased's wife above and below the cliffs on the left side of the beach. The sea, with tidal access to the cove was at the bottom of the page.

"Any one of them could have shot the deceased, sir," South said morosely. "It doesn't look as if a stranger stood a chance of entering the cove without being seen."

The senior officer puffed out his cheeks. "My instinct says it was someone who's in this house right now, but it would have been tight. Eight people all in the area at the same time and all with a motive, I should think. Although, I've a mind to discount James Allington. I don't think he's got the brains to do it and I'd be surprised if he has a motive really."

His father spoke. "I think it's unlikely to be him," he agreed, "but he's what I call a gatherer. He watches and listens, and that can make a man dangerous. I'd watch his back if I were you because he may have seen something and not realised it."

"You could have something there, Dad. Make a note of that, South. We may have to get specialist help to prise any information from that man. It might be a good idea to get Barton on to Zach Allington. I want to know the man's past

45

and present and whether he has any more enemies, although I think we have enough to contend with, with the suspects here."

"And here's me thinking this was going to be a straight forward murder, sir," South said sullenly. "I suppose we'd better get our people on to the suspects' pasts as well. It sounds like there's going to be a lot of skeletons in the cupboards, and that all takes time."

"Well it doesn't help that people will lie," Adam said forcefully. "That Reverend for instance. He was hiding something, and no doubt the rest of them will as well. They just don't realise that we will rout it out in the end. Still," he gave a resigned sigh, "that's police work for you."

"Well at least we know they all had the opportunity, so just motive and means to go; although I think uncovering means and motive won't be difficult with this lot. South, get Collins to help Barton and after that get Mrs Peaceful in here. If we don't get a move on with these interviews we'll be here all night," Andy instructed. "Oh, and South, round up the rest of the statements as well please."

After he'd left the room, father and son moved over to the patio doors and gazed into the garden. It was quarter past five, yet the air was still sticky and sweet, with the scent of the sea, flowers and a hint of the farm on top of the hill. Zach had been dead nearly five hours and Adam was thoughtful. He said, almost to himself, "I've met Zach a few times, you know. Can't say I liked the man. Brash, common sort of fellow. Lucky though. From what I can recall he was on the brink of bankruptcy when his partner died. That lottery ticket couldn't have come at a better time. But he knew things, son. You heard what the Reverend said about James. Well the same could be said about Zach." He turned back into the room and the two men stood face to face. "Zach was like the devil. He could reach right into your soul, and then he would tease and torment you with his knowledge." He shook his head causing a stray strand of hair to flick over his eyes. "A 'revelation party' though? Strange. I don't understand it. Was Zach really going to stand there and just tell everyone what he knew? Damn dangerous and foolish thing to do, don't you think?"

Andy tapped his fingers on his teeth. "A man has a dream or a godly vision, whatever you call it, and calls eleven people together. We know and they know that he was going to give a substantial amount of money away." He shook his head and sighed. "But how does that affect the guests? I mean obviously the family are going to be shocked, but the guests?" He cogitated for a moment and sat down. His father crossed the room and sat down opposite. "So on the one hand the deceased has a divine intervention which has the effect of making him change his ways, and yet on the other hand, he wants to expose peoples' secrets. Something good. Something bad. It's confusing me, Dad." He shook his thoughts away. "Anyway, let me clear my mind for the moment and talk of other things. Tell me about this woman. By the twinkle in your eyes I'd say you think she's something special."

His father chuckled. "Evangeline," he crooned. "A lovely name for a very nice lady and definitely not a murderer. At least not in my eyes. If the murder took place around about twelve forty then I can alibi her. We boarded one of those charter boats about eleven and we were out at sea for about an hour and a half. We were the only two passengers and got talking. We found we had a lot in common so the next step was a bit of lunch. She was with me the whole time until we arrived here about four forty-five.

"So she was with you during the relevant times? Well that's good, Dad. At least that's one person off my list," Andy said.

"I should hope so. I'm a good judge of character as you know. She was only on the boat to kill time. She wasn't due to arrive in Priest's Finger until later this evening, so she caught the Jurassic bus from Exeter and stopped off at Lyme and I'm glad. She's very nice, Andy."

Andy smiled. "I'm glad too, Dad. Now what about…"

Before he could carry on the door opened and South proceeded into the room followed by Mrs Peaceful. She entered the room with the same arrogance as her husband and without being invited, sat down in the chair that Adam had just vacated. Andy noted that she was a lot shorter, more rotund, and probably quite a few years younger than her husband. She'd dyed her hair some time ago because her roots now created a two inch grey seam from her scalp, changing to a dull henna. It hung lankly, its straggly ends clinging damply to her flushed cheeks and forehead, framing a portly, unpleasant looking face. Here, eyes a light brown, bulbous nose and thin lips formed a determined triangle, yet her skin was wrinkle free and creamy coloured. She wore thick round glasses.

Her stare was as direct and unflinching as her face, as Andy introduced himself, South and his father, the latter affording him his past Sergeant title. He consulted the statement placed before him. It was presented in longhand but fortunately the constable that had written it up, did so in bold print making it easy to decipher. "Muriel Peaceful. Born sixth of the twelfth 1963. Married the Reverend Peaceful in August 1991. So you have been married nearly twenty-three years. Your husband tells me you moved to Priest's Finger three years ago. Where did you live before that?"

She answered in a surprisingly quiet, birdlike voice. "Until I married Ian, I lived with my family in the village of Little Grantham just on the Dorset-Somerset border. My father was the vicar of St Gregory's. Ian had just been given a small but thriving parish of St Matthew's in Hammersmith. We remained there until four years ago, it was about Christmas, or thereabouts, when Ian decided it was time to semi retire. We were offered a small cottage at a very reasonable price, here in this village, with the proviso that he would offer his services in a couple of the outlining parishes. Ian liked the idea of settling down and writing a novel and here we are," she finished with a dissatisfied glance around the room.

"You prefer the hustle and bustle of a busier town?"

Andy presumed.

Muriel affected a shrug which was barely discernible under her baggy brown dress. She must be uncomfortably hot, Andy thought. The fabric of the dress seemed to be made of some kind of linen and billowed around her body like a half-inflated balloon. He brought his attention back to her voice. "I had my friends there, a knitting circle and the WI. Enough to keep me busy. I have nothing here, as you can imagine."

Andy could well imagine. Her discontent hung like a grey cloud, heavy about her stooped shoulders. "How did you feel about Mr Allington?"

"I met him a few days after he bought this house. I actually liked him," she admitted with a slight shrug. "He was kind to me. I was kind of lonely and so was he, I think." She gave a hollow self-deprecatory laugh. It was oddly childish. Andy found himself feeling sorry for her. He didn't think she had a fulfilling lifestyle. He looked at her statement. Unbelievable to see that she was actually quite learned. A Licensed Lay Minister Doctor no less. Her talents obviously drowned under her husband's ambitions and personality.

"When was the last time you saw Mr Allington?" he asked. It was the most repetitive yet necessary question that was asked with every incident.

She considered the question in a slow and measured way. Her eyes wandered round the room seeing nothing. A couple of minutes lapsed. In the same slow fashion, her gaze settled back on him. "Certainly not today. Yesterday I suppose."

"You didn't go to the cove this morning?"

Muriel Peaceful lowered her eyes. "I admit I was going to, Inspector. By the way, is that the correct way to address you? I'm afraid I have had little contact with the police."

"That's perfectly acceptable, Mrs Peaceful or should I call you Doctor?"

"Perhaps we should carry on as we have," Muriel Peaceful suggested.

"So may I inquire what your movements were this

morning?" Andy asked. He was getting tired of the questioning now. It was a long time since he'd eaten anything substantial and he always found the initial questioning thoroughly boring.

"Well you see. I followed my husband this morning. It was about twelvish. He went down to the beach…"

"From which direction?" Andy interrupted.

"From the manor actually. We left our own home at about eleven with the intention of seeing Jennifer, to ask if we could help in any way for the party later on today. That was Ian's idea not mine. We ended up arguing as usual. I didn't want to go to the party, I don't think Ian did either, but there you are." She shrugged. "Not that that will be happening now. Thank goodness. I don't like parties, Inspector," she explained. "Especially this type of party. A revelation party, for heaven's sake. There were times when Zach could be such a fool. It was pretty obvious that someone was going to do something. You can't go threatening to expose people and take away their money and remain unscathed. Can you?" She stopped abruptly.

"Did you kill him?"

"Not that I expect you to believe me, Inspector, but no, I didn't."

"You say you followed your husband, Mrs Peaceful. Why was that?"

"I thought at first he might have arranged to meet Jennifer but then I decided that he must be trying to talk to Zach. I admit to being a little surprised when I saw Ian disappearing into the cove. If there was one thing you can be sure of with Zach it was that he hated, no loathed, being disturbed when he was in that cove. He could be quite insufferable about it."

"So why would your husband arrange to meet Mrs Allington?" Andy was confused. "And also, why Mr Allington?"

"It's called a woman's instinct, Inspector. I have reason to believe my husband and Jennifer are having, or are going to

50

have, an affair. I've seen them together on several occasions. You know what it's like. The looks between them, little things. A woman knows. Whether his feelings are reciprocated is another thing. I have to ask myself what on earth Jennifer sees in Ian." Her voice had lowered as if she was suddenly thoroughly bored.

Andy gathered his thoughts. "So you followed your husband down to the beach initially because you thought he was meeting Mrs Jennifer Allington?"

Muriel looked disinterested and shrugged. "Yes, but I was wrong. It was Zach he wanted to see this time."

"You didn't follow him into the cove?"

"I've already said I didn't. I stayed beneath the canopy of trees and waited for him to return. After ten minutes I gave up and came back here. I thought I saw that young lady Felicity walking across the pathway towards the cliffs, but it was only a fleeting glance, and I could have been mistaken. It could even have been Jennifer I suppose. They're about the same height, but like I say, it was only an impression out the corner of my eye."

"Did you see anyone else this morning? Did anyone see you?"

Muriel sighed. She shook her head causing a damp strand of hair to stick to her forehead. "No one, Inspector. I didn't even see Ian return. As there was no one in the house I made my way back home. Ian came back about fifteen or twenty minutes later. It could have been longer I suppose. When I realised it wasn't Jennifer he was meeting, I lost interest."

DCI Fortune shuffled the papers on the desk. Everything she said sounded plausible, but like her husband, she was holding information back. She came across as a woman impervious to the suffering of others, yet he felt that underneath that inscrutable exterior, she was a cauldron, bubbling with emotion. Was she so indifferent? he asked himself.

"Statements will be drawn up for you and your husband

to sign, Mrs Peaceful," he said eventually. "Read it carefully then you can both go home. We will be talking to you again sometime tomorrow, so if you can make yourselves available please." He stood up. "South, escort Mrs Peaceful out and gather up the statements from Mr Crouch and Miss Battersby. We'll go through those before speaking to the family."

South returned shortly bearing the two statements. He read them through. Clearing his throat he began. "Percy Crouch, sir. Fifty-one-year-old farmer. Owns much of the land around here along with his son, Ben. Been in some conflict with the deceased for nearly a year. Apparently the deceased had been making advances to buy as much of the land as possible. Seems the deceased was trying to build himself a right little empire. You know the kind, sir. Little pond. Big fish." He pulled at his shirt where his collar was slowly gluing itself to his neck. "Mr Crouch and his son were both invited to this evening's party. Neither was looking forward to it, in fact, Mr Crouch insists it was unlikely they would be going. Too much to do on the farm was his explanation. At the relevant time Ben, the son, was in the fields helping stack the hay bales with a couple of farm hands. Mr Crouch was in his barn repairing some machinery. He says he thought he saw James Allington crossing his land but can't be too sure." He looked up. "That would tie in with James Allington going down to the cove, sir. It would have taken ten to fifteen minutes to walk from the back of the house, over the fields, let's say about twenty-five past twelve or thereabouts."

Andy marked the time on the sketch. He nodded. "Yes. That's about right, but he still had time to nip down to the cove and kill Mr Allington. Our James is not a reliable witness and probably didn't notice him. I think he had his own agenda in his head, though heaven knows what it was. And let's not forget that the deceased was going to do or say something to the farmer tonight. Was it worth killing for I wonder? Anything else, Bill?"

"No not really. He says he was busy and it was loud in the barn so he didn't hear anything. He vaguely remembers a bit of noise out at sea, those jet skis he thinks, but the machinery was on and maybe a helicopter crossed over the farm about half past twelve. All rather haphazard if you ask me," he grumbled.

"Andy remained thoughtful for a few moments. "What else have you got?"

"A Miss Battersby, sir. A spinster. She's lived in Priest's Finger for twenty-odd years now. She used to be a teacher in one of the Bridport schools and retired when she moved here. She's seventy-two and by a strange coincidence, knew the deceased when she taught in a secondary school in Hammersmith. Says she didn't kill Zach but wished she had."

Andy and his father raised their eyebrows simultaneously at this remark. "Seriously, South? Is that what she said?"

"Yes, sir. She also said he was a repellent little bugger and the rest of his family was just as bad. She had no time for any of them. She particularly disliked James. Said he was an obnoxious creep and she wouldn't trust him as far as she could throw him. She saw him about twelve fifteen walking by the woods. He was loitering on the path. He wandered off when she headed into the woods to go mushroom picking."

"Mushroom picking, Bill?" Adam asked. "What kind of mushrooms?"

South looked down at the statement. "It doesn't say. Is it important?"

"Not really," he answered. "As our victim was shot it hardly matters at all, but had he been poisoned, well…"

"I see where you're coming from, Dad," said Andy. He rubbed his hands together. "At this juncture I think it highly unlikely that a seventy-odd-year-old woman went running towards the cliffs and fired a shot, without being seen. Was she also invited to the party tonight, South?"

"Oh yes. It says here she had every intention of going as well, which is a bit strange if she hated them all."

"Well then, South. We'll get on to the family now." He turned to his father. "Why don't you take your Eve away for a few hours while we tackle the rest of the questioning? Maybe you can find out what she knows and why she was invited tonight. Her husband fell, and I say that lightly, from the cliffs at Ringstead some two years ago. Perhaps she has some suspicions about the accident but whatever, see if she will open up to you."

His father didn't look too happy about it and nodded reluctantly. "I'll see what I can do and, Adam," he asked, "you'll keep me informed won't you?"

"Cross my heart, Dad," he said following his words with actions. "We'll talk later on at our hotel. We're staying at the Cork and Funnel near Bridport so meet us there about nine."

Adam Fortune left, shutting the door softly behind him. Andy and South remained in the middle of the room. Andy sighed tiredly and rubbed his stiffening neck. "Okay, South. Let's get the widow in here."

Chapter Four

Eve sat alone at the table and sipped her coffee. She was mostly ignored and had been since she'd slipped quietly into the lounge. Jennifer and Felicity sat side by side on the sofa talking in muted tones, while Michael paced up and down. Occasionally he glanced towards her in confusion but rarely acknowledged her. Eve felt very much alone and superfluous. On previous visits she'd had the same feeling, one of being an unwanted guest. Zach, however, had always made her feel welcome but still, she thought, she shouldn't have come. The small note enclosed with the invitation had been most insistent though. She remembered it word for word, yet slipped the note from her bag and read it surreptitiously.

Please come, my dear Evangeline

Eve hated the way he used her name in full but that was Zach. So pedantic he emphasized everyone's given name. His pedagogic quibbles about grammar were well known. The note went on:

I need you by my side. Something has happened, something dreadful yet so uplifting. You must listen to what I have to say. It is to your advantage, yours and Julian's. He visited me, you know

Eve didn't know. She would have a word with her son when he arrived.

Showed me something powerful of which I am so ashamed. I should have realised the truth, my dear, but I'm a selfish, stupid and greedy man. I closed my mind to the obvious and now I need to make amends.

Once again, Evangeline, I need you. Please come.

The door opened and James sidled in. He looked furtively around then went and sat down by the patio doors. He showed a blatant aversion to his family and turned his face away from them, staring out into the garden. Eve studied him. Of all the family it was James she was most offended by. There was something really bad about him, there always had been. Not a lovable child or adult, he made her skin crawl. Harsh thoughts which made her feel guilty and ashamed, but she had no control over her emotions where he was concerned. She'd tolerated him for Wendy (she'd had a great deal of affection for her late friend) and Zach's sake, but Eve couldn't stand him. Every now and then James' body would give little jerks and his head would shake uncontrollably. A creepy laugh, a sly glance round the room yet he was ignored by everyone bar herself. It was impossible to have any sympathy for his condition, though. In fact, it was Zach whom Eve had felt sorry for. He'd tried his best by James, he really had, and in his own way, he'd loved his youngest son.

Zach had been a good family man. With Wendy he had been different, a much kinder person, more tolerant but her death had changed him and Eve felt that by marrying Jennifer he had made a bad move. There was no love between the two women, they both held a deep seated resentment towards each other.

Eve had grown up with Zach and had eventually married Clive a few months before Zach's marriage to Wendy. The partnership between the two men had at first flourished but hard work had been no defence against the rising effect of a world-wide recession. Clive had become more introspective and began spending more time in the office. Acrimonious words between the two partners had erupted frequently. When workers had to be laid off, the animosity between the partners bit into their already fragile relationship. In those last few weeks she rarely saw Clive and when she did, they often argued bitterly into the early hours. It was a horrible time. And then Clive had died. Thrown himself from the top of the cliff into a raging sea. Without warning she had become a widow with an angry disagreeable son. Had Zach not won the lottery and provided a share of his winnings to them, Eve didn't know how she would have managed. Zach had provided a constant allowance to keep her afloat and paid off the huge deficit that was her mortgage. Eve was sure that Jenny resented her husband's generosity, but Eve had been in no position to refuse the money.

And now, here she was back in the house she vowed every time never to visit again. This time though she had an ally. A dear, wonderful man who had made the journey to Priest's Finger, with its malevolent house, bearable. Somewhere close by, Adam was with his son and somewhere close by, Zach lay cold and lifeless on a mortuary slab. Murdered.

Anger suddenly burned inside her. Where was the grief? The tears of loss? Not in this room that was for sure. Zach could be truly obnoxious but he didn't deserve to be killed. She would mourn him, the man who had been a friend to her, her lifeline, and she wouldn't rest until she had received retribution for him. It was a callous murder and with Adam's help they would find his killer. How she knew this, she didn't know, but Adam was once a policeman and they would work together. She would make sure of it.

A discreet knock on the door brought her out of her reverie. A uniformed officer poked his head in. "Mrs Allington? The Detective Chief Inspector would like to see you now," he requested.

Jennifer Allington stood up. Although the same age as Eve she was a lot more beautiful. Expertly made up and wearing an outfit that must have cost a fortune, and which would have looked ridiculous on Eve, she gazed haughtily around and practically glided out of the room. The pernicious atmosphere lessened, and surprisingly Felicity, who had stringently ignored Eve, sent her a shy smile. Eve returned the smile and with a pat on the chair indicated to the young girl to sit with her. Her relief was evident as she slipped quickly to Eve's side. A quick hug was exchanged before the door opened again and this time it was Adam who crossed the threshold. He gestured with his eyes that he needed her and with a sorry shrug to Felicity, Eve eagerly left the room.

DCI Fortune wasn't sure what he expected when Jennifer Allington entered the room but it wasn't the glamorous figure that oozed its way into the chair. She crossed long shapely legs and stared directly at him. She was exceedingly beautiful, he thought, but certainly not a grieving widow.

He knew her age to be fifty-seven but at first glance she looked a lot younger. Possibly in her mid-forties. Whether her looks were natural or artificially crafted, he didn't like to guess, but he suspected she'd been injected with some kind of synthetic material. With the best will in the world maintaining a frown-less forehead was next to impossible. She continued to stare at him with a slight smile on her lips. He was intrigued. What was a woman with her looks doing with a man like the late Mr Allington? He'd seen the man and even though he was dead at the time, nothing could disguise the general ugliness of her husband. They'd married long before he'd become a rich man though and they'd had a daughter together so perhaps her husband had once been a handsome man. She hadn't married him for his money anyway. That had come after years of unlikely wedded bliss, he thought.

"When did you last see your husband, Mrs Allington?" he inquired. Normally he would have offered condolences but he felt they would be wasted in this instance.

"I saw him to talk to about ten o'clock this morning. He came into my room to ask for some last minute information regarding the party. The last time I saw him was when he was on the beach. He could have been dead or sleeping," she added indifferently.

58

"You don't seem particularly upset," he observed. "Were you not on good terms?"

She gave a patient sigh, a slight breath that lifted her breasts. "You probably know a great many details about our lives already, but for your information my late husband had been going through some sort of godly transition, which has upset the running of our household of late. Zach wasn't an easy man to live with in the best of circumstances. No doubt you have heard what kind of person he was. To put it bluntly, he was a bore and an arrogant bastard. He ran this household totally regardless of anyone's feelings but his own. Yes. We had money and abundant amounts of it but we had to live in this hideous monstrosity of a house in the middle of nowhere and our lives are miserable." She gazed off into the distance. "Trapped in this backwater," she murmured to herself. "All the trappings of wealth and stranded with village idiots as friends. Fliss and I wanted a city lifestyle, theatres, shows, shopping, Harrods, parties, real friends, but Zach wanted to bury himself in the countryside. Lording it over his own pathetic kingdom." She sniffed. "Well now we can move on. Sell this mausoleum and buy a nice property in London. Go back to where we belong." She faced Andy. "So, Chief Inspector, am I upset? No I'm not," she said defiantly. "Zach and I have not lived as man and wife for many, many years and before you ask, no I wasn't happy about his damned epiphany," she snorted. "What wife would be? Giving our money away. Not a bloody chance."

Andy took a steadying breath. "So you went to the beach and killed him then?" he asked bluntly.

The look she sent him was cold. "I went to the beach I admit. But kill him? No I didn't."

"Did you see anyone else whilst you were there? The Reverend Peaceful maybe?"

"Aah Ian. Yes he was there," she admitted casually. "He went into the cove to see Zach, though heaven knows why. Zach hated being disturbed and enjoyed being left in peace when he was in that silly little cove. His own private little world you see. Master of all he surveyed," she added derisively.

The callous disregard of her husband's life rankled Andy. Yes she had a pretty face but Jennifer Allington had a deep rooted ugliness that showed itself every time she opened her mouth. He amended his earlier thoughts. Now he wondered what the murdered man had seen in this woman. He bit back his anger. "I see from your statement that you were on the opposite side of the beach when Ian Peaceful went into the cove. Why didn't you show yourself to him?"

She gave him a sultry smile which now failed to impress him. "Ian has rather a thing for me, Detective," she confided. "You've met Muriel haven't you? Rather a dowdy creature, don't you think?" She preened, flicking her curly blonde hair. Something else artificial, Andy thought watching the way the colours caught the light. She carried on talking. "It always amazes me that women don't make the best of themselves. How do they expect to keep their husbands?" she said with disdain. "His feelings were not reciprocated however, and I thought it best to remain hidden until he disappeared from sight. I thought I would get a chance to speak to Zach before he came back here but after waiting for quite a while and no sign of Ian returning, I crossed the beach and sneaked round the rocks and into the cove. Ian wasn't there. He must have gone over the top."

"And your husband, Mrs Allington. What was he doing? Did you speak to him?"

"Zach was asleep or possibly dead in his chair," she said callously. "I went over for a quick peek but thought I heard someone coming, so I left him sitting there and returned by the other path and cut back through the fields to here."

"So you are saying that after all the trouble waiting on the beach to see your husband, you then decided at the last minute to leave him there without saying a word?" he asked disbelievingly. "You didn't think to check that he was okay?"

Jennifer pulled her short cardigan over her shoulders. "I've already said that I thought I heard someone coming. I needed to speak to Zach in private and that wasn't going to happen. I didn't want to speak to him in the house. As you are aware we were supposed to be having a party tonight, and with all the activity going on and guests arriving, a discreet conversation was out of the question."

"So what was so important that it couldn't be said in the house?"

She laughed harshly. "Zach was going to give our money away. I needed to stop him. Nothing was more important than that. Foolish man."

Andy ignored the last comment. "And you're saying that your husband was asleep?"

"Certainly, Detective," she said heartlessly.

"Not dead with a hole in his head then?" he asked sarcastically.

Jennifer was not amused. "I think I may have noticed that, had there been one."

"And you are sure you saw no one else either before or after you left the cove?"

"Quite positive," she asserted. She stood up and straightened her skirt. Her tone was dismissive. "I have important things to do, Detective, so if there's nothing else?"

Andy decided to let her think she had the upper hand and also stood up. "Thank you for your time," he said untruthfully. "We will need to speak to you again, and after we have interviewed your son and daughter we will be leaving but we will be back early tomorrow morning." And with South opening the study door, he dismissed her. She went out without a backward look.

"Phew. She's a nasty one, sir," observed South after she was out of earshot. "Mr or Miss Allington next?"

Andy checked his watch. It was nearing six. "Let's get the daughter in now, South. It appears from her statement that she turned up at the house just before the murder. Not that we know the exact time the shot was fired, but it would be nice to eliminate someone else at this stage of the game."

He resumed his seat seconds before Felicity was shown in

the room. Unlike her mother there was a guilelessness about her. His father's brief synopsis of the family had formed an opinion in Andy's mind that the youngest member of this dysfunctional household also had several personality imperfections. What was it he'd said? That she was a selfish, spoilt little brat and in league with her mother.

Andy wasn't so sure. There was certainly a slight resemblance to her mother but the hardness hadn't yet taken hold. He knew that she had left the family home some months before and moved to London. Perhaps time away from her family would enable her to grow without her mother's strong influence. She smiled at him and once again he was struck by the lack of grief this family showed. He began questioning her. "I see that you arrived here about twelve. What did you do then?"

She had a soft voice. "I called out but the house was empty. I was a bit peeved that there was nobody to meet me as I said I would be here about eleven, but I was stuck for ages in Weymouth due to traffic, so I suppose everyone got fed up with waiting."

"And then?"

She shrugged and swung her head round to look out the patio doors. A wisp of scent reached his nose. "I went to find Daddy," she said simply.

"Did you enter the garden through the lounge?"

"No, I came in here, just in case Daddy was on the phone or looking at his guns. He goes into a world of his own sometimes and doesn't hear a thing. He wasn't here so I knew he must be in the cove, so I went across the garden towards the cliff path." She pointed in the direction of the doors.

"What happened then?"

"Well I had a few problems." She lifted up one leg and showed her high heeled shoes. "These to be precise. Bloody things kept catching on the brambles. I could barely walk."

"So how long did it take you to get to the cove?" he probed.

Felicity took a moment before answering. "About twenty minutes I suppose. I do remember hearing someone coming so I hid behind some bushes. You see, I wanted to have a word with Daddy about something and I didn't want to be overheard."

South shuffled in the background and Andy leant forward, elbows on the desk. "Did you see who it was?" he asked hopefully.

Felicity shook her head. "No. Whoever it was passed quite close to me so I put my head right down so I wouldn't be seen."

Andy looked across to South and the latter shrugged. "Okay," Andy sighed. "What did you do next?"

"I left it about five minutes or so then got up and went to the cove."

"Right, you reached the top of the steps that lead down into the cove. What then?"

She tipped her head to one side. "Nothing happened then. I could see Daddy sat in his chair facing the sea just as normal, and I called out to him. He couldn't hear because of the helicopter hovering overhead. When it moved away I called again but Daddy was dead to the world." Her hand flew to her mouth. "Ooh," she cried. "Was Daddy dead then?" She shook her head, her fair hair flaying across her face. "Of course he was. No wonder he didn't answer," she finished lamely.

Andy closed his eyes briefly. "You didn't go down to him then?"

Once again she raised one leg. "In these. I don't think so," she added ironically. "I got fed up with waiting so decided to talk to him later and came back here."

Andy decided to be open with her. "We believe your father was shot in the head by one of the guns missing from that cabinet. You admit to using this room to get to the garden. Did you notice anything out of the ordinary? Were the cabinet doors open for instance?"

She looked around. "I didn't notice. I had other things on

my mind at that time."

"What was so important that you needed to speak to your father as soon as you arrived?"

Felicity heaved a weary sigh. "I suppose I'd better tell you. It will be out in the open soon enough." She took a deep breath. "I got married yesterday. To Julian Traversy. I wanted to tell Daddy first. He wouldn't have liked it and would probably have gone mad, but when Mummy finds out she's going to hit the roof. She can't stand Julian or Eve. The shit's going to hit the fan when she finds out," she shrugged indifferently. "Oh well. Look, officer. I've been on the road for hours. I'm tired, grubby and starving. A shower is waiting for me. Can I go now?" she sounded fed up.

He relented. "Okay, that's it for now. We will question you further tomorrow so don't leave the house till we tell you please."

She gave him a grateful smile. "I won't, don't worry. I'm going to have a long soak and an early night. If I'm not in the house when you return, look for me on the beach. It would be a shame to waste this weather." With that she left the room.

South came and sat down in the seat she had just vacated. "Well she's a calm one. What do you think, sir? Could she have killed him? We only have her word that she was wearing those shoes and what's to say she didn't take them off and go down. She's a young woman. It shouldn't have been too difficult."

"I agree, South. We're going to have to question James again, though whether we'll get any sense out of him is another matter. What else did he see? Something must have alerted him to go into the cove. From what I can gather he was prohibited from going down those cliffs but he did in the end. What did that man see I wonder, and will we ever find out?"

South sighed dramatically and looked at his watch. "It's twenty past six, sir. Shall I get our final witness in? I need some food." With that his stomach gave an affirmative grumble.

'One may smile and smile and still be a villain' were the words that popped into Andy's head when Michael Allington sauntered into the room. Shakespeare's lines aptly described the man's persona. Although nothing as yet had been pulled from the police records, here was a man who had certain attributes of a criminal. He was too casual and there was a certain awareness in the pale eyes that revealed that this wasn't the first time he'd been in the presence of the police. Andy invited him to sit down. "I won't offer words of condolence, Mr Allington. I haven't met anyone in this family who seems particularly upset about the death of your father," he said bluntly, "so I'd like you to tell me about your movements today."

Michael Allington still smiled, showing a line of straight white teeth. "Well I got up about ten thirty and had my usual three course breakfast. Coffee and two cigarettes," he added jokingly. He gave a nervous laugh when neither officer responded. "Then I took the car into Bridport for an hour for a mooch around, getting back here about a quarter to twelve. I was going to have a drink in the house but I heard voices in the lounge. Peaceful and his wife were there. They were having a bit of a barney so I left them to it and went down to the beach. I sat on top of the cliff and smoked for a while and that's it really."

Andy closed his eyes and remained thoughtful for a few moments. "So how long did you sit there for?" he asked.

He consulted his watch. "I suppose about an hour. I'll admit right now that I wanted to have a word with my father but it was like Piccadilly Circus on the beach. My stepmother was just below me hiding behind some rocks, the Peacefuls were lurking by the cove, the wife of that strange relationship was hiding in the trees. I think she was spying on her husband. That dirty excuse for a man of hers has been sniffing around Jenny, though heaven knows why. She'd never entertain a man like him. He gives me the creeps so God knows what he does for my stepmother. My father seemed to like him though. They spent a lot of time together locked up in this study." His eyes wandered vacantly around the room. "I suppose Jenny will get rid of this now," he mused. "She always hated it."

"So you didn't go into the cove then, Mr Allington?"

He waved a dismissive hand. "Call me Mike for God's sake, and no I didn't. Like I said, there were too many people about. Even old farmer Crouch was out of his farm and that old hag Battersby was rummaging in the undergrowth by the woods. I did see a car though," he added with a sly grin. "A big silver thing parked at the top of the lane in the lay-by. Could that be your murderer?" he asked hopefully.

Andy looked across to South who gave as negative nod of his head and rolled his eyes. If what Michael Allington was saying was true, somebody unknown was also in the vicinity. Andy groaned inwardly. He was hoping there wasn't going to be any outside influences but with the man's statement things had suddenly become more complicated. "We will look into that in due course," he said. "So let's get back to the beach. Did you observe anyone go into the cove?"

"Oh yes. I saw the Reverend go in about twelve fifteen, I think his wife remained in the trees. I'm not sure about Jenny though. I did look down again but she'd gone. Couldn't say what time. I'd laid down for a while trying to catch some rays so she could have gone to see my father. Who knows?" he shrugged. "There was that much activity going on it was difficult to place where everybody was and anyone could have sneaked into the cove from the other side. There's plenty of bushes and trees and enough pathways leading back here, or to the main road without being seen."

Andy stood up and walked round the table. He positioned the rough map they had drawn and placed it in the centre of the desk. He pointed to one of the red crosses. "This is you, Mr Allington. Your stepmother below you. The Reverend Peaceful and his wife, the latter in the trees and the former by the edge of the cove. All the other crosses indicate the position of the rest of the family and farmer Crouch, his son Ben and Miss Battersby. You say the silver car was where?"

Michael gestured with the tip of his finger. "About here."

Andy marked it with another red cross. "Does the layout seem about right to you?"

The other man nodded. "I think so, although I didn't see Fliss or James at the time. They must have arrived on the scene when I was lying down."

"Quite so. Well let's talk a bit about your late father," Andy said returning to his seat. How would you describe your relationship with him?"

"BC or AD?" Michael asked.

Andy frowned. "I'm afraid I don't understand, Mr Allington."

He laughed throatily. "Before Christ or after. I'm sure you know all about his epiphany. My father was two different men. Before his so-called vision he was a tight-fisted old coot. Oh don't get me wrong, it was easy to get money out of him but he wasn't what I call savvy with his loot. He spent his money like water but he drip-fed his family. He kept us all tied to his purse strings but he didn't ask too many questions about how we were going to spend it. This house cost a fortune and then there were the donations to the art circle and the local political party and God knows what else. He had visions of a knighthood, you see. His money was a pathway to the elite society, as he called it. And then there was the man after his epiphany." Here he paused for breath and gave a deep sigh. "It's amazing how much a man can change just because he'd had some sort of vision. It was bad enough that he spent so much of it on rubbish but suddenly he wants to give it away," he said with a disgusted snort. "I just don't understand it. No more cash for any of us and then to rub salt in the wound he decides to have a bloody party to announce his decision in front of everyone. A 'revelation party'. What the hell is the point of that?" He stopped suddenly and lapsed into a morose silence.

"Did your father ever talk to you about the rest of the guests invited tonight?"

"No." He shook his head. "Why would he? We all knew them."

"We have reason to believe he was going to make a few statements tonight. Not just about the money but he was going to reveal some secrets. Secrets that someone might kill for."

Michael's face brightened at this. "Really? Well I'll be damned. Although it wouldn't surprise me in the least." He raked his fingers through his hair dislodging the gelled strands of his fringe leaving pointed spikes sticking in the air. There was a slight tremble in his hand and he gripped his knee. He leant forward eagerly. "You know something, Dad liked to know things," he confided. "Even with us. 'Where have you been?' 'Who have you seen?' 'What did they say?' 'What were they doing?' Endless questions. But that was just his way. Research I suppose. Liked to keep one step ahead. Scared that someone might know something he doesn't." He moulded himself into the leather chair and raised his eyes to the ceiling. He frowned. "I can see it now," he said thoughtfully. "That was probably why he kept the Peacefuls close by. I mean they're hardly scintillating company but they were in and out of this house like bloody yo-yos. And why the old hag and Crouch tonight?" He smiled wickedly. "I'd love to know what their secrets are." He lowered his eyes, leant forward and put his elbows on to the polished desk. "What a pity someone killed the old coot," he said callously. "Looks like he or she ruined a bloody good party."

Chapter Five

Adam found a little cafe he knew by the seafront in Burton Bradstock, and Eve had forced herself to eat a sandwich even though she wasn't hungry. Only at Adam's insistence had she swallowed her food. They walked for a while afterwards on the pebbled beach but both were restless to see how the investigation had progressed and decided to go to the nearby town. It was nearer eight when she and Adam entered the lounge of the Cork and Funnel. It was a quiet rural backwater pub situated on the edge of the bustling town of Bridport. Like most pubs, it had evolved into a popular eating place and was well served by the populace and holiday makers, who enjoyed the countryside ambiance.

Andy and South were seated at a round table in the corner by the bay window finishing the remains of their surf and turf dinner. Over the meal they had discussed their day and put in place their agenda for the next day, and were now deliberating the pros and cons of their prospective football teams. South was an avid Fulham fan whilst Andy supported Arsenal.

They stopped their dialogue when Adam and Eve sat down in the vacant chairs. The pub was heaving but most of the punters congregated near the bar affording the four a quiet and secluded area to talk privately.

Eve sat down on the hard-backed chair facing the window. Adam and Andy fought their way to the bar for a round of drinks. She was tired now. It had been a long day and the death of Zach weighed her down. She gave a tight smile when her glass of wine was placed before her but she remained silent. Pulling her cardigan over her shoulders she let the muted conversation wash over her. Poor Zach, she thought. Poor wonderful, stupid Zach.

She felt a nudge on her arm and came to with a start. She looked around and shook her head. "Oh sorry," she said. "It's been a long day."

Adam patted her arm and looked into her eyes. They

were the kindest eyes she had ever seen. "You're tired," he said apologetically. "Shall I take you back to the house?"

Eve shook her head. "Don't be silly. I was just daydreaming. I was thinking about Zach. It's so very sad and to think one of them killed him. Unbelievable."

Andy spoke then. "Eve? Oh sorry. Can I call you Eve?"

She nodded. "Of course. What do you want to know?"

"Why were you invited to the party tonight?" he quizzed gently.

Adam tensed beside her and she laid her hand over his. "It's alright, I don't mind answering any questions. I want justice to be done and someone in that house killed Zach." She delved into her handbag and brought out the letter. She handed it across to Andy. He read it quickly. "I received it last week. It doesn't really explain anything but that was Zach for you. He obviously wanted to tell me something." She sighed deeply. "But I haven't a clue what it was." She looked around the table. "I hate going to that house. Jenny can't stand me. I think she disapproved of Zach giving me money from his lottery win, but I was really grateful. After Clive died I was destitute. We'd re-mortgaged the house to prop up the business and I had Julian at home, who at that time wasn't the nicest of men. My world fell apart. Without Zach's generosity I would have lost everything." She lapsed into silence reliving those first dreadful months.

"And the rest of the household?" Andy prompted.

She broke out of her reverie. "Fliss and Michael were always polite when I was there, but I don't think they cared one way or another. James on the other hand…" She paused and chewed on her fingers. "I hate saying this but… I don't like him. Never have," she admitted looking at the men one at a time. Her cheeks flushed as she tried to explain. "He's devious, sly and manipulative. When he looks at you it makes you feel vulnerable, kind of exposed if you can understand that. It's nothing tangible, just feelings I suppose." She sighed gently shaking her head. "And doesn't that sound awful? It's just that he makes me feel so uncomfortable. I think Zach was the only one who loved him without question. And of course, Wendy," she added.

"His first wife?" Adam asked.

Eve smiled at him. He was rather nice, she thought and she felt such an extraordinary connection to him. It was a strange feeling, bearing in mind she hadn't looked at another man since Clive had died. Yet she didn't feel awkward or uncomfortable in his presence. It was as if they'd known each other for a lifetime. She spoke to him directly, her brown eyes staring into his green eyes. "Wendy was lovely," she said carrying on with the conversation, "and Zach was a different man then. Oh don't get me wrong. He was still a bit of a bully and definitely the force behind the business partnership. He could be quite brutal sometimes and many a time I'd seen Wendy with unexplained bruises on her arms. But she loved him unconditionally and although I tried to intervene, Clive always warned me off. At first I thought Zach had had something to do with her death, in fact, at one time I was sure of it. Jenny and he were as thick as thieves, even back then. I thought they were having an affair and so I suspect did Wendy, but after Wendy died and nothing happened, I thought I must have been mistaken. It was a few years later that he married Jenny and had Fliss, but those niggling doubts have never fully left me. My own fault," she smiled wryly. "I always did have a suspicious mind."

Everyone smiled kindly. "Did you meet the neighbours, the Peacefuls, Mr Crouch, Miss Battersby, etc.?" Adam had taken control of the questioning. His son and South sat back in their chairs and listened intently, the former happy to let his father take over the investigation for the moment. Mrs Traversy certainly seemed comfortable and more open to the questioning.

Eve grimaced. "Yes I've met them all at one time or another. I don't like the Peacefuls very much. They're a funny couple and totally mismatched but I saw so little of the farmer and Miss Battersby that I can't form an opinion, negative or positive. Zach knew them very well though. He once told me that he went to the same school as the Reverend and that Miss Battersby used to be his teacher. Whether that was in the same school I can't say." She shrugged. "I can't tell you anything else unfortunately."

Adam squeezed her hand and Eve felt comforted. From across the table came a little cough. Eve tore her eyes away. She frowned. Adam's son looked uncomfortable. Eve unhooked her hand from Adam's, even though that small contact felt so natural. She reddened with embarrassment. Obviously Andy wasn't reconciled to his father being even slightly affectionate in public. "Sorry," she mumbled feeling guilty.

Adam opened his mouth to intervene but Andy held up his hands. "It's alright, Dad. I just need to interrupt and ask Eve a couple of questions. I don't mind the hand holding, in fact it's nice to see you so happy." His father eyed his son reflectively for a few moments then took Eve's hand again. She didn't resist.

"What is it, Andy?" she asked.

South and he exchanged a quick glance. Eve held her breath. "Your son Julian?"

Eve looked confused. "Yes?"

"We know he's been invited to this evening's postponed party?"

"Yes?"

"What time was he supposed to arrive?"

Eve thought for a bit. "Julian phoned me this morning. He said he was leaving Southampton about ten and was expecting to arrive about four this afternoon. He had a couple of calls he needed to make on the journey."

"What car was he driving?" he inquired.

Eve felt a lump in her throat. She put her hand on her breast. "Oh my God," she gasped. "Has something happened? Has there been an accident. Is he alright?" She could barely breathe as she stared at Andy. "Please," she begged.

"No, no, no," Andy reassured quickly. "Nothing like that.

It's just that we need to know his whereabouts. There has been some news about your son but at this juncture it's nothing that we can reveal. I'm afraid that information needs to come from him," he said mysteriously. "No. We just want a know something about his car. Make, colour, etc.?"

She barely heard him. Although it was still light outside, her reflection stared back at her from the curved pane of glass. A haggard, worn face confronted her. 'The face is the image of the soul' were the words that popped into her head. Was it Cicero who said that? she wondered. If it was, then never more truer words been spoken. By the gaunt look on her face her soul was still badly damaged by the past. Her eyes looked wild and bulging, paralysed in time, by fright and the unknown. She remembered the feelings of shock when they'd found Clive, battered beyond recognition on the rocks at the bottom of the cliff. It all came back with dreadful clarity.

"Eve. Eve?" a voice penetrated through the fog that clouded her mind. "Good God, son. What have you done?"

She heard the voices and calmed her breathing. "It's okay. It's okay," she stuttered. "Sorry, I'm so sorry. He's alright isn't he?" she beseeched.

A glass was pushed into her hands and she took a grateful sip. The cold liquid eased her throat. She focused on Adam. She trusted him.

"He's fine, Eve," he promised.

She believed instinctively and nodded her head. "The police asked the same thing when they found Clive," she explained shakily. "He'd taken his car to the cliff you see. We don't know why. It was only five minutes from the house. One minute we'd just finished dinner and were sat talking round the table. Jenny was making the coffee in the kitchen. All perfectly normal. The next minute Clive got up from the table, said he was just popping out for some fresh air and threw himself off the cliffs. It just suddenly came back to me." She shook her head, her brown hair flaying from side to side. "I feel such a fool," she said angrily. "I do apologise.

73

It's a silver grey Mondeo," she added calmly. "It belongs to the company he works for."

"I know there's a good reason for your question, Andy," Adam said impatiently, "but what is it?"

Eve noted the look that passed between the two men. Adam spoke again, his honest eyes caressing her face. "You can speak in front of Eve, son. She's not on your list of suspects and I won't keep anything from her."

She felt her heart melt, just a little, and looked expectantly towards Andy and South.

"You might as well tell me. I'm going to do all I can to help you find Zach's killer. With your father's help of course." She felt rather than saw Adam's nod of agreement. "You might not like it but that's tough," she added forcibly. "So go on," she urged.

Andy gave a wry smile. She could see that he knew he was beaten. "Around the time that Zach Allington was murdered," he confided, "Michael Allington, the dead man's eldest son was, allegedly, sitting on the cliff top. He says that a large silver car was parked at the top of the hill in a lay-by. If he is telling the truth then there is a likelihood that your son Julian was the occupant of said vehicle. Obviously we need to investigate further, inquiries are ongoing but we have a couple of constables at Priest's Finger Manor. We haven't received any news as of yet, re his arrival."

Eve was nothing if not persistent. "And the other news that you're withholding. Can you tell me anything? A hint perhaps?"

Andy shook his head stubbornly. "No unfortunately not. That's a private matter between you and your son I'm afraid," he said cryptically but smiled to take the sting out of his words.

Eve leant back and gave him an intense stare. "Okay," she nodded. "I'll let you off for the moment. So what can you tell about your investigation so far?"

It was Bill that gave them a short summary. "They've all admitted being in the area at the relevant time, but of course, nobody has admitted shooting him. That withstanding, we haven't met any suspect who seems the least upset about Mr Allington's death. In fact it appears to be a very convenient death for all concerned."

Eve shook her head sadly. "I agree. It makes me so angry that they're so indifferent, that Zach's death is so insignificant. He wasn't totally bad you know," she said forcefully.

Although Adam disagreed with her, he squeezed her hand reassuringly. He wasn't about to reveal his own personal feelings regarding the dead man. "I'm sure he wasn't, Eve, but I think we all concur in that you can offer some really insightful observations that will help move this inquiry forward. If you want to that is?" he added.

"Oh you can definitely count me in. This was a brutal murder of someone who helped me out when I needed it most. Don't get me wrong though. I had no illusions about Zach. He could be quite churlish at times and crude." She looked thoughtful for a moment. "Yet he wasn't always like that. At least I didn't often see that side of him, but I sometimes got the feeling that he had a bad childhood. That something made him bad."

"You do realise, Dad, that you will have to investigate without any police backup," said Andy. "Officially you have no standing and you need to be careful. Someone in that village is a murderer and there's no telling what might happen if the killer thinks you are getting close. We can pool information though and anything instructive in the reports I'll pass on to you – on the quiet of course."

Adam stared at Eve, a query in his eyes. She nodded to his unasked question. He turned back to his son. "We'll be careful, Andy. Eve and I will conceive a plan of attack which will probably involve lots of talking. She knows quite a lot about these people. She's actually staying under their roof and I'm only up the road from her."

"That's true," said Bill. "Can I ask your opinion on the deceased final words while we're here? We can't make head nor tail of it. James Allington told us that his father's dying words were 'his call'. His call to do what we wonder? His call to die or be killed? It just doesn't make sense."

The four of them sat quietly with their own thoughts each mulling over the conundrum of those two small words. In the background glasses clinked at the bar, conversations were muted and the sweet chords of Yanni's 'One Man's Dream' drifted appropriately to their ears. Eventually Adam broke the silence. "It doesn't make sense," he agreed. "Certainly the man I knew wouldn't have instigated his own death. He was far too proud and arrogant to do such a thing but this epiphany thing is a whole different ball game. He became a changed man. You would have thought that if a man found God, he would only want to do good. He certainly wouldn't want to die. The whole idea is preposterous."

Andy sighed. A deep lethargy engulfed him. It had been a long day and the heavy meal followed by a couple of lagers settled heavily in his stomach. He yawned tiredly. "I think I'll sleep on it for now, although there's one thing I'm sure of. This was a deliberate case of premeditated murder and nothing will persuade me that this man invited his own death. Whoever killed him took the gun from that cabinet with murder in mind."

It was nearly ten when they left the pub so that the two police officers could retire to their beds. Adam folded Eve's arm through his as they strolled along the road. Now and then they stopped and looked into the windows of the small, select shops that dotted the high street. Although the trauma had left her drained she knew she would have a hard job sleeping that night. She was so keyed up. The fact that she had to go back to the house, certainly as an unwelcome guest, added to the strain she was feeling. Thank God for Adam, she thought.

She took a sly glance at the man at her side. He had a nice face, she thought. Sort of calm and reassuring with just a hint of nobility. A sharp nose with a slight bump between his eyes was the only imperfection she could see. The contours of his face were well defined, no sagging jaw lines of loose chins you'd normally associate with the older man. Even his skin retained some of its smooth, youthful appearance. He was a good six inches taller than herself, much stockier than she really liked in a man, her late husband was thinner and wiry in stature, yet by the feel of his arm and from what she had observed, unobtrusively of course, he seemed fit and strong and Adam appeared to carry no excess fat. The limp in his leg was less pronounced now than when she had first seen him, making his way on to the charter boat. Then, he had lowered himself on to the deck with a stiffness in his leg and a wince of pain which clouded his eyes. Their eyes had met and he had been the first to offer a shy, tentative smile.

Talking had come naturally then. Two strangers sitting side by side whilst the small boat glided over the calm blue sea. She couldn't remember the commentary about the wonders of the Jurassic coastline that had accompanied their journey. They'd been too busy making friends with each other. It seemed so natural to go to lunch afterwards and then meander along the main street in Lyme Regis. They had both enjoyed the shops full of fossils and skeletal remains of long lost creatures that had once roamed the earth all those thousands of years before. She sighed deeply. It had been a wonderful day until they had arrived at Priest's Finger.

"Worried about going back to the house?" Adam queried looking down at her.

His genuine concern lifted her spirits. "A little," she admitted. "If I didn't know you were close by, I would probably have found myself a hotel somewhere though," she admitted.

"You can always stay with me," he offered hesitantly and quickly added, feeling that he was being a bit presumptuous. "There's a spare room available with clean sheets and I can always go to the house and pick up your overnight bags."

Eve squeezed his arm. "That won't be necessary, Adam.

If we're going to investigate Zach's murder then one of us needs to be in situ. And it might as well be me."

Adam looked down at her face. She looked so earnest and confident. Her dark eyes like pools of liquid chocolate brightened visibly. Gone was the dull pallor of tiredness replaced by the alertness of a terrier. The symmetrical line of her face, surrounded a pixie-like nose and the cutest most kissable lips while her skin was pale, smooth, and blemish-free, bar a slight hue that rouged her cheeks. He thought she was simply gorgeous, that the simplicity he saw in her eyes was deeply attractive. For the first time since his wife had left him some twenty years previously, he felt a long forgotten flicker of excitement.

He was not really convinced with her line of reasoning though. He was sure the murderer was in that house and he didn't like the thought of her all alone with the suspects. But in the short time he had known her he'd seen her inner strength and knew instinctively that she wouldn't do anything stupid. "Okay but please be careful."

"I promise and besides, Julian should be there now and it sounds like he and I need a chat. I'd like to know why he went to see Zach. There was no love lost between them. I've always believed that Julian thought Zach knew a lot more about Clive's death than he admitted."

They had turned the corner, making their way back to the pub where Adam's black BMW was parked. "And what do you really think about your husband's death?" he asked cautiously. "Was he the type of man to commit suicide and in such a gruesome way?"

Eve was thoughtful for a while. She'd never spoken to anyone about the death, not even Julian. For months afterwards they'd both been stunned by grief, neither one able or willing to delve too deeply into their feelings. And when, much later, Eve felt ready to open up it had been far too late. An invisible barrier of doubt and speculation had grown between them. Unbreakable. Unclimbable. The lack of communication, especially on her part (she was his mother after all) still made her feel guilty and somewhat inadequate. She should have known what to do and say. Failure didn't sit easily on her. Finally she said meditatively, "No matter how desperate our situation was, Clive always tried to remain upbeat. In his own way he was quite strong and far more optimistic about the future than I was. He always believed that something would turn up. 'Let's see what tomorrow brings', he would always say. Then a couple of months before that fateful night he started to change. He became secretive, would disappear at odd times in the day and night. I'd go to bed and wait for him and hear him go out in the early hours of the morning." She shrugged half-heartedly. "I never knew where he went or what he did, yet, even though we were in deep financial trouble and we were about to lose everything, I'm still shocked that he killed himself." She paused for breath, stopped and looked directly at Adam. "He hated heights you know, even though he was a builder. It was always Zach who climbed the ladders and dismantled scaffolding. Clive mostly remained at ground level mixing cement and doing the heavy manual labouring. The strange thing is if he'd swallowed a load of tablets, maybe I could have accepted it. But throw himself off the cliffs? No. Definitely no," she said shaking her head so vehemently it dislodged some of the grips holding her hair in place. Her emphatic denial made her statement totally believable.

"The police were quite sure it was suicide?" Adam questioned.

Eve nodded. "What else could they think? There were no witnesses and with all the problems Clive was having, and the fact that we were well on the road to ruin, they were quite positive it couldn't be anything else. They say the wife is always the last to know but Clive and I grew up together. We were friends first before becoming husband and wife. I truly believed I knew him better than he knew himself." She sighed sadly, a look of bewilderment on her face. "It just goes to show how wrong you can be."

Adam reacted spontaneously and pulled her close, enclosing her in his protective arms. "Stop blaming yourself, Eve. It was never your fault. No one knows what goes on in a person's mind, no matter how well you know them." He tried to be reassuring but he'd seen enough suicides and the devastating effects it had on the loved ones left behind, to know the misery of never knowing the answers. All the 'what ifs' that lasted a lifetime.

Eve relaxed against his shoulder. "I know you're right," she mumbled. She pulled away from the comfort of his arms. "Come on. I need to get back to the house before they lock me out. I wouldn't put it past Jenny to barricade the door," she laughed.

"And you'll be okay?" he sought reassurance.

"Come on," she urged, tugging his hand. "The sooner I get there the better."

The drive took twenty minutes and when they arrived it was obvious the occupants were still up. Julian's silver car was parked on the gravel alongside three other cars. Turning the engine off they heard loud voices, raised in anger as they walked the path to the back garden. There were so many voices shouting over each other that it was difficult to make out the context, but as Eve opened the door she heard Jenny's strident voice carrying over the others. "You're lying!" she screamed. "You're just like your mother. Nothing but a free loader. Parasites, the pair of you. If it wasn't for Zach giving you money neither of you would have given us the time of day."

Another voice this time. It was Fliss and she was screeching at the top of voice. "Stop it. Stop it."

Eve had had enough. She tore away from Adam and stormed into the lounge. At a glance she saw Julian striding up and down the room. Fliss was pulling at his shirt. Michael and James sat stunned, watching warily from their seats on the sofa. Jenny had her back to the patio windows and she was fuming. Her eyes blazed at Julian such hatred and loathing.

"What's going on?" Eve asked quietly. Her voice was deadly calm.

Jenny turned on her. "Bitch. You lying, rotting, cheating bitch," she shrieked with such venom that the room went quiet. Julian stopped pacing, Felicity stared wide-eyed and petrified. Michael dropped his head and stared at the floor. James mumbled and rocked back and forth.

Adam tried to move in front of Eve but she forestalled him with a wave of her hand. She directed her stare at Julian. "What's going on, son?" she asked sternly.

He was waving small flaps of pink paper in the air. "This, Mum," he cried. "I was in the attic going through Dad's paperwork and I found these in Dad's diary. They're lottery tickets. Dad's lottery tickets. He used the same numbers every week. Six. Twelve. Eighteen. Twenty-three. Thirty-seven. Thirty-eight."

"I don't understand, Julian. What does that mean?" Eve demanded.

Julian took a deep breath. He stopped pacing and stared directly at his mother. He was sweating heavily, his breathing was harsh. Felicity took his hand and held it tightly. She stared at him with a worried frown. The air was still, the silence was deafening. Julian took another deep breath. His voice shuddered as he spoke. "On the night Dad died, his numbers came up. I checked on the computer." He shook his head. "Zach didn't win the lottery, Mum. Dad did."

Nobody said a word until Adam spoke. "But if that's true why did he kill himself?"

"Don't you see?" cried Julian. "Zach must have killed Dad. How else did he get his hands on the ticket? Zach's a murderer, Mum. And I can prove it."

"You greedy fucking bastard," Jenny cried venomously. "Not just content with trying to steal our money with your disgusting lies, you had to go and marry my daughter. Seems to me you were hedging your bets. You grasping son of a bitch."

Chapter Six

Nobody had any sleep that night. The house fairly vibrated with anger all through the hours of darkness and it wasn't until the rising sun peaked over the horizon that Eve fell into a deep yet restless sleep. She awoke at eight, heavy-headed and dry mouthed. She was tempted to bury her head under the quilt but the hollow feeling in her stomach forced her from her bed and into the bathroom. She looked into the cabinet mirror to confront an image she barely recognised. Her face looked haggard and careworn, her skin grey, her eyes sunken, her lips pale, her wrinkles more pronounced. My God, she thought, I look older than my mother did on her death bed. She flashed a handful of cold water on her skin and walked slowly back into her bedroom to slip into light beige slacks and a flowery patterned T-shirt.

Downstairs in the dining room all was quiet. The patio doors were open and a cool breeze wafted gently in. On a small table in the corner lay cups and saucers and a large carafe of coffee. She poured herself a cup and stepped outside. She needed to think, to sort out the muddied thoughts of the night before.

So Zach had really murdered Clive. What an unbelievable scenario. He must have slipped out on that fateful night, followed her husband or enticed him outside somehow. How long would it have taken to push Clive over the cliffs? More importantly how had he lured Clive up there? Everyone who knew Clive knew how much he hated heights. He'd never have gone up there willingly. Zach must have said it was something important to get him out of the house.

She thought back to that evening. Both Jenny and Zach had left the table on different occasions. Making the coffee, clearing the table, going to the bathroom, and that sort of thing. Zach had taken a few calls in his study. Hadn't he said something about some paperwork that needed signing? She racked her brains.

Clive had left the room about eight. To get some fresh

air, he'd said. He'd had a bit of a headache but had he been acting strange that evening? she wondered. Eve couldn't remember everything but she tried to visualise Clive, sat at the head of the table. Yes. She recalled after a few moments. There had been something subtle, a sort of nervousness tempered with excitement. An atmosphere of anticipation had settled insidiously over that table that night and Clive had definitely been agitated about something. At the time she'd put those little nuances of his behaviour down to him committing suicide, but what if it was to do with having the winning lottery ticket? Her thoughts floundered and she took another gulp of coffee.

Concentrate, Eve, she urged herself. Hashing up the past was agonising but it was crucial to get to the truth. For Clive's sake. She carried on with her thoughts.

She did remember that she'd been alone at the table for nearly twenty minutes before Jenny came back carrying a tray of coffee. After that, or was it before that? she'd gone upstairs to change, after spilling coffee on her dress. She must have been gone at least fifteen minutes arriving back in the dining room in trousers and a clean blouse.

It could have been longer though, she thought with hindsight. Worries about the business and the house being possessed may have clouded her memories. After all, she'd had a huge shock when the police arrived. When Clive had been missing over an hour Eve had insisted that they were called. It hadn't taken long to find the abandoned car, just at the end of the track. Just a few feet from the edge, where his body had fallen on to the jagged rocks below. It had been Zach who identified his battered body later that evening.

So presumably Zach had got in the car with Clive, and obviously Clive had shown him the winning ticket. Zach must have snatched the ticket and in one terrible moment of sheer greed, pushed Clive over the edge. It would have been over in minutes. Zach had been a healthy fit man and would have run back to the house in a few moments, pretended he'd been on the phone, then casually waltzed back into the dining room. A freezing wave of grief washed over her. Dear God, how could he?

Zach, with his insatiable desire for power had murdered not only her husband but his best friend. All of a sudden Eve's desire to find his killer waned. In a brief moment of madness she wished that it had been her who fired that fatal bullet.

She blew out a long heart felt breath. And what of Julian and Felicity? she wondered.

Abbotswood police station was set just outside of the village on the main A3157 road that took the car traveller towards the town of Bridport. The station itself was still housed in the multi-gabled Crofton Manor. Originally built in the 16th century, it was extended in the 17th century. Its mullioned windows and steep, stone-slated roof were heavily preserved by English Heritage and although the inside had changed somewhat, the outside facade of the building remained unscathed by time.

There was a muted conversation going on in the incident room when Andy and Bill entered the room. Andy walked across to the window and looked over the paved courtyard which was now used as a car park. The window was opened fully, but the breeze was barely detectable, not even a breath of air to stir the branches on the trees that edged the road. In the distance he heard the soft sound of a tractor somewhere out in the fields and a car crossed the bottom of the driveway. Without the sound of people outside, Andy felt a deep isolation. He was used to the hustle and bustle of the city, and was still finding it hard to adjust to the intimacy and the smell of the countryside. He turned away from the solitude and faced the room.

Barton, Collins and Townsend sat at the back of the room while their assorted male and female colleagues either stood against the wall or occupied the remaining chairs. Andy sat on the corner of the deck and Bill South went over to the board in the corner by the window.

On the board was the enlarged photograph of the deceased and also other photographs of the layout of Priest's Finger Manor and the surrounding area. Somebody had had the foresight to take a frontal picture from the sea, which clearly showed the two coves and the back of the house.

"Right everyone, let's have your attention please," South said vigorously. He rubbed his hands together eager to get on with the day. Immediately the room went quiet. "You can see where all our suspects were at the time of the murder. The red crosses mark their respective positions and an approximate time." He looked around the room at the attentive faces. "Some of you have timed how long it would take to reach our victim and they are as follows: Reverend Peaceful. He arrived on the beach about twelve fifteen. He's an agile bloke for his age and could have been in and out the other side of the cove in about eight minutes. He has admitted climbing up that cliff face on a number of occasions in the past. He's a rum sort of bloke and we believe that our victim had some sort of hold over him. We have a witness who saw him go over the rocks into Funnel Cove. His wife also attests to that fact.

"Muriel Peaceful. A licensed lay minister no less. Was also in the vicinity at the right time. Could easily have followed her husband into the cove and although there were no witnesses to this fact it doesn't mean she didn't go there. Again, the timing is right and we estimate it could have taken her about ten minutes. Can't imagine what sort of hold our Mr Allington had over her but that doesn't mean there wasn't one.

"Jennifer Allington. Wife of the deceased. And not a very loving wife either," he added. "She was also in the cove in front of the house here," he pointed with a finger to the red cross. "She was crouched behind some rocks and was seen by her eldest stepson, Michael, who incidentally, was sat above her on the cliff edge. Again we estimate about ten minutes for her to cross the beach, shoot her husband and leave Funnel Cove by one of the two paths that rise out of the cove." He cleared his throat and took a sip of water. "Mrs Allington openly admits her contempt for her late husband and comes across as greedy and manipulative. She has a strong motive to get rid of him so bear that in mind.

"Michael Allington. Eldest son of the deceased. Would have taken a bit longer to get to his father. Maybe about twenty minutes or so, but still possible within the time-frame. No love lost between father and son and our suspect was certainly upset to hear his father was about to give away a substantial amount of money. We've checked the police database and have no record of anything serious about him, but rumour has it that he's well in debt and has a bit of a drug problem. He needed money so we need to check his background and bank account to see what's going on."

He turned and addressed his boss. "Everything alright so far, sir?" he asked.

DCI Fortune nodded his head. "Carry on, South," he said grimacing. "But let's move it along as quick as possible." He felt his collar and pulled it away from his neck. "It's stifling in here." There was a murmur of agreement as the sun rose and blazed through the window. South hurried along, squinting his eyes.

"Felicity Allington. Says she arrived at the manor about twelve. Admits to entering the study so could easily have removed the weapon. She left the house via the study doors and made her way to the cliff edge of Funnel Cove. No witnesses admit to seeing her but the ground at the top here," again he pointed to the layout, "as you can see is overgrown with plenty of bushes to conceal her. Says she heard someone passing her about twelve thirtyish so hid in one of said bushes. Could have been the Reverend or her mother. Again the timing is crucial and needs to be thoroughly checked. She broke the news to the family last night that she'd recently got married to one Julian Traversy. We'll get on to him in as minute. Not too sure what her motive could be at the moment but that's no reason to rule her out. News of this marriage has certainly put a spanner in the works as I will explain in a minute.

"James Allington. You've all got his statement in front of you and I know some of you officers have met him. He doesn't make a lot of sense as you can see. From what we can gather from his statements, he left the house by the front, crossed over the fields by Badger Woods, and skirted over the grassland belonging to local farmer, Percy Crouch, to the top, far right of Funnel Cove. Why he went down into the cove to see his father we don't know but something must have alerted him to do it. We will be asking police officer Kelly to talk to him as he has expertise in this area. What he heard doesn't make any sense but he said his father's last words were and I quote: 'his call'. Get your brains round this ladies and gents and get back to me asap with your ideas. Seriously though, we don't think James is a suspect but his life may be in danger. He's been described as a man who's devious and sly and possibly quite secretive so we need to watch his back." He blew out a breath. "Now let's go on to the next two suspects who we think are out of the frame." He took a sip of water.

"Percy Crouch. As I said before, local farmer and along with his son was invited to party that should have taken place last night. He was only five minutes away from our victim. Neither heard nor saw anything and says he was working in the barn with machinery going. On paper it looks like he has nothing to do with the murder, but Zach Allington had been trying to buy up his land and had also been making financial inducements to his son Ben. So something there we need to look into, folks.

"Miss Battersby. Definitely not a serious contender. Although in the right place at the right time. She's in her eighties and with the best will in the world there's no way she could have moved quickly enough to kill our man and get out of the cove and out of sight. Still, we need to delve into her past to find out about her relationship with Zach. It may have no bearing on his death, but it may give an insight into

Zach's character." South moved about to stretch his legs before coming back to the board. He pointed to the top of the map.

"Julian Traversy. Our final suspect." He sighed deeply. "This is a tricky one. His car was spotted at the top of the hill parked in a lay-by on Wilmott Lane. Turns out he's not only married to our Felicity, daughter of the deceased but, and here's the crunch. He arrived at the manor a couple of weeks previous, accusing the deceased of the murder of his father, one Clive Traversy who, it was alleged at the time of his death, threw himself from the cliffs near Ringstead. The police closed the case when facts emerged that Mr Traversy had serious debts from the business and was possibly going to lose his home, which was heavily mortgaged to prop up the company's finances. Now it turns out that, after going through his father's effects some weeks ago, Mr Julian Traversy had found a number of lottery tickets with the same numbers that won Zach Allington the princely sum of seventeen million pounds on the Euro lottery. There's a considerable possibility that our dead man committed the murder of his business partner and friend. And what this means, folks, is that Julian had a very strong motive. Like all our other suspects he also had means and opportunity."

DCI Andy Fortune stood up then and addressed the room. "Thanks, South. Any questions? No. Right. Let's get on to our victim. In front of you, you hold most of the details we have collected so far, so we won't go over them again. What we need to do now is look at the character of the late Mr Allington." Andy crossed his arms. "New information has come to us overnight which you have only just been made aware of. It looks like our corpse took a shortcut to fame and fortune. Two weeks ago Julian Traversy found lottery tickets that seems to prove that Zach stole that winning ticket. He immediately approaches Zach and we can only guess what followed that conversation."

"Excuse me, sir," Barton interrupted from the back of the room, "but if this Julian murdered our man why wait so long?" He screwed his face up. "I mean, the poor bloke's just found out that not only our dead man killed his father but also stole a massive sum of money. If that was me I wouldn't wait two weeks for him to arrange a bloody party. It doesn't make sense does it?"

Andy nodded his head in agreement. "Thanks for your observation, Matt. We'd pretty much come to the same conclusion ourselves. Which bring us to our man's character. He's been described to us as a bit of a bully. Self-centred, arrogant, acquisitive, and quite possibly a blackmailer. Not for money you understand but he had a penchant for secrets." He squeezed his bottom lip between thumb and forefinger. "And yet, confronted with his own well-kept secret he decides to throw a party. A 'revelation party' he calls it. He tells everyone he's had some sort of epiphany and then decides to gather family and acquaintances from the village for an evening's entertainment in the manor."

"Sounds like he was going to have some sort of confessional to me, sir," said George Collins.

"He doesn't sound like a Catholic to me," South smirked. "My ex-wife was one of those and she spent more time with the local priest than she did with me. Never did get to thank him for all the earache he saved me."

General laughter filled the room and even Andy managed a tight smile. "Yes well. Thanks for that, Bill." He wagged a finger. "You could be on to something though, George. We know that the family knew he was going to give a lot of money away but that wouldn't have affected the rest of the guests." He looked thoughtful. "So was he going to expose secrets or promise never to use those secrets again? Perhaps he was going to say sorry to everyone."

"Doesn't sound like the Zach Allington I know, sir," said a gruff voice from the front of the room. It was Sergeant Parker, a man of long-standing service, and someone who had worked in Abbotswood well over twenty years.

"Care to explain, Jack?" remarked Andy.

Parker sat straighter in his chair and rested his hands on

his round belly. After much thought he began. "I was in the area when the Allingtons moved into the village. He was a bad one from the start. Complained about the road being too narrow to begin with. First day he wanted the lane widening, he'd had a huge removal lorry. Then it was the trees, the neighbours, the smell of the farm, the noise of the tractors and the mud on the road. Just endless grousing, sir. All I can say is that it must have been a huge epiphany 'cause that sort of man don't change his ways. Not in my opinion anyways."

"And yet he did change according to his family. And it was a change that got him murdered," said Bill South.

Andy considered. "I can't help feeling just a mite uneasy about this case. We've got a lot of suspects, they've all got means, motive and opportunity and most important, luck. Each suspect had a window of opportunity of about five minutes. Now by my reasoning if all of our suspects entered the cove with the intention of killing Zach, one had the gun obviously, then we can't reach the conclusion that it was the last person who visited him, killed him. If you were going to kill a man and he was already dead when you got to him, there's a good chance you would walk away and pretend he was asleep, as several of our suspects attested to."

There was silence in the room until Collins spoke up. "Shall we divide into our usual pairs, sir, and do house to house inquiries?" he asked awkwardly.

Andy and Bill stared at each other. Andy was desperate to put his own stamp on the station but at the same time was loath to interrupt the smooth running of the operation. He'd been keenly aware of how the men and women worked together in this smaller outfit and so far no serious problems had arisen. But still, over the next few months he intended to supplement new ideas and build new partnerships. Supplanting the ex-DCI, even on a temporary term wouldn't stop him reinforcing his own authority. So far he'd been flexible, but his team needed to get used to working within different teams to stop the staleness slipping in. For the moment though, he and South would keep a watchful eye.

"Okay. Carry on as you normally would do," he said promptly. "DS South and I are going to Priest's Finger to re-interview the family. I want background checks done on everyone and results on my desk by the time I get back. Those of you on house to house go over the statements of the Peacefuls, Miss Battersby and Mr Crouch." He dismissed them and walked out of the room followed by South.

Chapter Seven

Andy and South stepped through the open doorway and into the square hallway of the late Zach Allington's home. South called out but received no reply. They could hear a voice coming from behind the closed door of the lounge and without knocking, entered. Michael Allington, talking on his mobile, turned with a baleful glare, muttered something into his phone before placing it on to the table.

"Don't you people ever knock?" he asked insolently. He sauntered cross the room towards them and sat down in one of the high-backed chairs. He was wearing pristine white shorts and shirt of designer quality. Clean shaven, his dark hair groomed and immaculate, Michael Allington pulled out a pouch of rolling tobacco and proceeded to make a cigarette. The cheaply rolled up cigarette was at odds with the sophisticated image he was obviously trying to portray. He gave a casual wave to the other vacant chairs facing him and blew smoke circles above his head. "Feel free to smoke if you want to. My stepmother hates it but she's unlikely to be down for some time. She needs her beauty sleep," he added with a smirk.

The two men sat down. "No thank you, Mr Allington. We don't smoke but we would like to ask you some more questions and review your statement."

"Oh for God's sake call me Mike," he said waving his arm, causing grey ash to drop on to the cream coloured carpet. He seemed unaware and carried on drawing on the thin white tip. He gave every appearance of relaxed indifference when DS South straightened in the chair and began the interview.

"We prefer to keep thing on a more formal basis for the time being, Mr Allington."

"Whatever," he said rudely then snorted. "I should be used to that by now. My father could never bring himself to call me Mike either. He was always so bloody anal about names. It was always Michael, Felicity, he even called his wife by her given name. It was never Jenny or sweetheart, it was Jennifer this and Jennifer that. He made our names sound so damned derogatory," he ended peevishly.

South cleared his throat. "Has your relationship with your father always been so difficult? What about when you were younger?" he asked.

Mike sat back with exaggerated nonchalance and crossed his legs. He flicked the remains of his cigarette accurately through the patio window. "There was a time I suppose, when you might describe our relationship as quite close. Up to about five years ago we got on reasonably well. The company was struggling even then, but it was plodding along. I was working part-time in the office. He was hopeless on the computer but I was pretty good, if I say so myself." He shrugged. "Jenny dealt with clients and the paperwork, answered the phone etc. and I did a bit of networking and designing. All tickety-boo. Then the crash came and you know the rest."

"Not quite, sir. What happened after your father won all that money?"

He laughed out loud. "Ha ha. What a joke that's turned out to be. Here we've been treating Julian and Eve like poor relations and it's been their money all along. No wonder my father turned into such a bastard. He's just a common murderer. And now look at us. Poor as church mice. What are we going to do now?" he whined. He looked around the room with a bereaved expression. "I hate this house and I hate this backwoods village, and the people around here stink as well. It's been like living in a farmyard." He sighed. "The money's been nice though. You can bear anything when you have a credit card that never gets refused." He shook his head mournfully. "I should have known it was too good to last."

"And why's that, Mr Allington?" Andy asked putting his elbows on his knees. He waited patiently for an answer. His suspect chewed on his lip and stared into space. "Perhaps you knew that your father had killed Clive Traversy and stole the winning ticket?" he suggested deliberately.

The silence in the room was as oppressive as the heat outside on the patio. The rising sun bounced off the concrete slabs and was so fierce it stung the eyes. Mike jumped noticeably. "Not true," he shouted. "Not true. Not true," he reiterated. He ran an agitated hand through his hair, heaved himself from the chair and paced the room. "How could I possibly have known?" he spoke to himself. "He just came into the room shouting and waving the ticket in his hand. Him and Jenny were dancing all over the place. Me and Fliss didn't have a clue what was going on. I must admit Dad did look a bit stunned but none of us disbelieved him. It was so surreal. We'd been skint for ages for God's sake. It was a dream come true. I mean, none of us even knew he played the lottery."

"He obviously didn't," South said brutally.

"No. He didn't did he?" Mike mused thoughtfully. "And what now?" he asked to no one in particular

"Mr Allington, if you'd like to sit down there is still the question of your father's murder to deal with," South said.

"Who cares about that now?" he cried bitterly. "He got his just deserts didn't he? Let's face it, who's going to go to his funeral? Not me for a start."

"Please sit down, sir," Andy said pointedly. "We would still like to know how your relationship changed when your father got rich."

Reluctantly, he sat down on the edge of the chair and fixed them with an angry stare. "I hardly see the relevance now." Neither officer offered an explanation and waited patiently. They didn't have the luxury of light clothes and both were uncomfortably aware of the overwhelming heat. South tugged on his shirt collar whilst Andy tried unobtrusively to loosen the grip his white shirt had on his sweaty back. They were aware of background noises signalling the waking of the rest of the household. Mike cocked his head. "The rabble are up then. Oh sweet joy," he said sarcastically.

Andy was losing patience. He was hot and stuffy and his throat was dry. Not a good combination. He checked his watch. Hours to go and he had a bad feeling the rest of the household were going to be just as surly. He had met with this type of resistance before but never had it been teamed with such blatant indifference. "The question, sir," he spat out through clenched teeth.

Mike sighed dramatically. "Crap if you must know. Suddenly he became the country man. Full of bullshit about us becoming members of the country set. He was a common builder for crying out loud. Living here in this damn great house with his immoral, self-indulgent ways. He tried to change all of us, turn us into fashionable members of society. Turns out he was nothing more than a bloody imposter." He flung himself against the back of the chair in angry disgust.

"Tell us more about yesterday," South said eying him steadily.

"My original statement stands, I've got nothing to add," he said bluntly.

"You're still saying you didn't go into Funnel Cove and confront your father?"

He looked at the two men with a hard, direct stare. "I did not go and see my father which is just as well. Had I realised what he'd done, I might have shot him myself. He's made bloody fools of us all and landed us in deep shit."

South was a born cynic and sent his boss a telling glance. He took over the questioning. "In your statement you stated that you remained on the top of the cliff and didn't move from there until the alarm was raised. Do you still abide by that?"

He was rolling another cigarette, the tip of his tongue sliding across the thin paper. His eyes were shielded from them but they saw the confident smile. He went to flick the lighter, thought better of it and stared at them with his dark gaze. His eyes then flicked to the door where high pitched voices could be heard getting closer. "My statement stands, officers. I didn't move until I heard a commotion. I then left my warm spot and made my way to the cove, where I met the rest of the family. I didn't observe anyone coming from the house but they must have heard from James. The police arrived just before the Peacefuls, and we all stayed there until we were moved by one of your constables. I have nothing more to add. I don't know if anyone saw me, that's something you will have to ask the rest of them." He rose from the chair, gave them a haughty look. "I must be going now," he said carelessly. "People to see, you know. Things to do."

Andy decided to close the interview. Better not to alert to the fact that there was ongoing checks into his background. As Michael Allington stormed out of the room, slamming the door behind him South looked at Andy and said, "He's going to be in an unhealthy position if things go badly with the money." Andy nodded philosophically.

Eve had just been about to set foot into the room when she heard Andy and Bill enter the lounge. Hearing Mike on his phone she'd held back and suffered in the cruel heat, forcing herself to remain in the inadequate shade, and eavesdrop on the conversation. The crunch of feet on gravel pulled her from the patio and round to the edge of the path. Adam stood there having walked the short distance from his house.

Now they stood on top of Abbotsbury hill, staring out over the clear blue water of the Fleet, and licking the welcome cold of their ice cream. There were a few tourists, like themselves, standing beside their cars, taking in the view. Andy took her hand and led her to the other side of the road, leading her up a well-worn path to a small hillside where they had a three hundred and sixty degree view of the sea from Exmouth through to the Isle of Portland, rising like a submarine from the water, to the far reaches of Osmington. They looked out over a panorama of hills and valleys, to the length of the A35 where they picked out cars travelling towards Bridport. Cattle, sheep and horses speckled the green belt of land in between. Turning full circle they gazed at the sheer, slate grey frontage of the steep cliffs, making up the impressive Jurassic coastline. Finally Eve looked down into the village of Abbotsbury, admiring the huge medieval tithe barn, where the monks of the ancient abbey received and stored their dues in produce, from the tenants who farmed their estate.

St Catherine's Chapel, built on a hill above the village some time in the 15th century was bathed in the strong sunlight and just down from there, the Swannery, where hundreds of mute swans, once bred for the monastery table, and now protected and allowed to breed in the shallow waters, spread like a white, downy fleece across the shoreline.

From their high vantage point they could hear the whispered sigh of the sea and catch the scent of salt and seaweed, the delicate taste of the former, drying their lips. Eve breathed deeply and felt a relaxing peace wash over her. For a brief moment in time she felt cushioned against the malignant feelings of the death at Priest's Finger, such a short distance away. She spoke in a soft whisper. "It's beautiful," she said facing him. "Thank you for bringing me here."

He was profiled against the dramatic backdrop, staring out with a benign expression towards the calm sea, glistening in the sunlight. The sun smiled kindly on his face, accentuating the strong, reliable silhouette, the sharp nose and firm jaw. His lips curved serenely as he stared out to sea. He looked cool and comfortable in his beige coloured shirt and light-weight shorts, seemingly unaware of the blistering heat. He closed his eyes, his long lashes fanning his cheeks and squeezed her hand. "I come up here quite a lot you know. When I need to think or to take stock of my life," he admitted. "There's something about this vast expanse of primeval landscape that puts everything into perspective."

Eve nodded understandingly. "I know what you mean," she said softly. "But you still can't escape your problems can you?"

"No you can't, Eve," he replied facing her. Her face was sombre. Like him she was an intensely private individual, loath to betray her innermost thoughts, but he wanted her to know that she could trust him. He could not think of a way to soften the blow of the words he was about to say, so said bluntly. "You realise that Julian is a prime suspect, don't you?"

Shock flashed in her dark eyes before she nodded reluctantly. "I know. I imagine that Andy will be interviewing him today and I'd rather be away from the house when he does that."

"Have you spoken to Julian yet?"

"No. I couldn't face him last night. It was a terrible shock when I found out he'd married Fliss without telling me, but to think he'd confronted Zach about the lottery ticket and not said a word to me about it sticks in my throat." She carried on sadly, "I hadn't appreciated how far apart we'd drifted since Clive died. Was I so unapproachable?"

Adam shook his head vigorously. "Don't think like that, Eve. Julian is a grown man. It must have been a terrible shock to him as well. Perhaps he felt that this was something he had to do for himself."

"It seems that he's more like his father than I thought," she spoke abstractedly. "Clive was always so secretive as well." They began to slowly descend the hill, all the while holding hands.

"There's so much to take in. I can't believe that Zach was such a phoney. He pulled the wool over my eyes. He fooled all of us. All those times when he gave me money, making me feel so inadequate and sort of grasping." She bit out angrily. "Do you know what I mean?" Adam remained silent and let her talk. She went on. "He was never generous with his money, not in his heart anyway. I always felt that he begrudged me those cheques, even though I defended him so rigorously last night. He could be nice yet he was also so bloody parsimonious sometimes, but I wasn't in a position to refuse. That's why I always stuck up for him." She shrugged resignedly. "I wanted to believe that he liked to help me, that he was doing it for his friend. How could I have got it so wrong?" she finished, shaking her head.

They'd arrived at the car. More tourists had turned up and the ice cream van was doing a roaring trade. Before Adam helped her into the car he said, "Do you fancy something to eat, Eve? I happen to know a nice pub in the village that does a good fried breakfast."

Eve smiled brightly. Despite the turmoil she felt she realised she was starving. "As long as you haven't made any plans?" she said.

"Only to spend the day with you," he laughed. "Better with you than spending the day alone or worse being in that house with that lot bickering and arguing."

Back at the manor, Jennifer Allington came charging into the room. Felicity followed and it was obvious that they were in the middle of a blazing row. They came to an abrupt stop when they saw Andy and Bill standing by the patio windows, the angry words dying on their lips.

"Well, well. This is a surprise," Jennifer said acidly. "Aren't you supposed to ring or something to let us know you are coming?" She crossed her arms and stared with vindictive resistance at the two men.

They were too professional to be intimidated by an angry suspect and stood their ground nonchalantly. "We did inform everyone yesterday that we would be here this morning," Andy returned placidly. "This is a murder investigation," he reminded her. "And it is in your best interest that we get this cleared up as quickly as possible."

"Well it's most inconvenient. I've just lost my husband, the house is in uproar and we have to contend with Julian and his ludicrous allegations." She uncrossed her arms but stood with rigid control.

Andy moved farther into the room and stopped a few feet from Jennifer. Felicity remained near the door watching carefully. "You don't believe your husband killed Clive

Traversy?" he asked casually.

Jennifer turned away from him and walked over to the mirror. She twisted her head from side to side smoothing her fingers over her cheeks and pouting her full lips. She'd obviously taken time, before leaving her bedroom, to put her make-up on. Her fair hair was pulled back and clasped with a diamanté clip, the effect accentuating the flawlessness of her skin and the absence of any fine lines that gave character. Medical enhancements had tightened the area around her lower jaw, highlighting the near-perfect symmetry of her face. She paused thoughtfully before turning back to face him. Her eyes were direct and ice blue. "My husband did not steal that lottery ticket, Chief Inspector, but as to killing Clive?" she paused deliberately and gave an affected shrug, "Who knows?"

Felicity cried out and confronted her mother. "How dare you say such a thing about my father!" she screamed. Her eyes were wild and accusatory. "You never knew how to be a good mother or a wife. He was a good man. He wouldn't murder anyone." Suddenly she burst into tears.

"Oh shut up, Fliss," Jennifer snapped crossly. "You don't know what you're talking about. You weren't around when Clive died, no one was. It was an accident pure and simple." She sighed irritably. "The police haven't a clue who killed your father so they are just using him as a convenient scapegoat. They're trying to say that your father killed Clive and therefore it follows that someone killed your father in revenge. It's ludicrous of course."

"So why say he did?" Felicity cried.

"Oh for God's sake, you stupid girl. I'm angry that's why. Zach has become as infuriating dead as he was alive," she said exasperated.

Her abasement of the man she was married to caused Andy to wince visibly. He squeezed his eyes shut and trained his face into calm indifference. Before he could open his mouth however, the door slammed open and Julian Traversy came charging into the room. "What the hell?" he exclaimed grabbing Felicity and closing her into his arms. Her sobbing increased with the added attention. Jennifer rolled her eyes and moved over to the patio doors by South. Andy quelled the urge to raise his voice to bring the room into order.

Julian had clearly dressed in a hurry. He wore the same clothes as yesterday and they were creased and had sweat lines from the heat of the previous day. His hair was stuck up chaotically, and his lower face unshaven. His eyes, so like his mother's, were dazed and sleep laden and he frowned with deep bewilderment. He held his wife at arm's length, hands on her shoulders. "What's going on, Fliss?" he asked gently. "What have they done to you?" He turned his eyes and stared hard at Andy for an answer.

"We haven't done anything yet, sir," Andy said patiently. "We've just come for a little chat and go over everyone's statements." He smiled caustically. "We would have preferred to interview you separately but as you are all together, I can't see a problem doing this while you are all in the same room. Unless anyone has any objections, of course?" Nobody replied but the anger and resentment was tangible. He turned to South and pointed to the other half of the room where there was a round glass table and six chairs. "We'll sit there and you take notes, South, but before we get started perhaps you can rustle up some coffee for us all?"

South left the room and Andy steered the reluctant family members to their chairs. Julian and Felicity sat next to each other holding hands, heads close together, whispering, while Jennifer sent scathing looks across the table at the couple. As soon as South re-entered the room carrying a tray of cups and a jug of milk, with a carafe of coffee the tension dissipated slightly. The steaming fragrance put a more social nuance on the room but still you could sense a wave of suspicious fear in the air. Time was taken while the social niceties were adhered to then Andy, after taking a few sips of the welcome yet scalding liquid, opened up a brown file which held copies of their original statements. South moved a few feet away and sat beside the door in an overstuffed chair and pulled out his notebook.

Andy began. "At this stage in our investigation I think we can rule out James as a suspect. After meeting and talking to him I don't believe he has the capability to remove the gun from the cabinet and with murder in mind, go and shoot his father. Not only does it not match with his intelligence but I can't believe there is any creditable motive." He looked around the table and received no response. He nodded his head. "Good," he said happy that no one chose to deny that assumption. "We have also ruled out the possibility of any outside influence, barring those in the vicinity – the Peacefuls, Miss Battersby and Mr Crouch the farmer. We know there were other guests invited to the revelation party, but they weren't expected until later on in the evening. They have also been ruled out. So that leaves four persons from the village and you Mrs Allington, you Felicity Allington, you Mr Traversy, and Michael Allington whom we have already spoken to this morning."

He put his elbows on the table, the statements between them. He looked down at the top one then up to Julian. "What time did you arrive in Priest's Finger?"

Julian still looked bleary eyed and half asleep. There was the tiniest whiff of alcohol as he took a deep breath and concentrated. His sigh was loud and exaggerated as he rubbed his finger over his lower lip. "I suppose it was about twelve fifteen. I thought I wasn't going to get here until later in the afternoon but my client had an urgent call away, so I set off straight here. I parked in a lay-by at the top of the lane for half an hour or so listening to the radio. Had some water." He shrugged. "And that's it really."

Andy picked up his pen and rolled it between his fingers. "Why didn't you come to the house then? You knew your wife had arrived I presume?"

He nodded his head. "Fliss told me she got stuck in traffic and didn't arrive until twelve. I didn't know that then of course." He squeezed her hand reassuringly. "She was going to tell Zach about our marriage. I did offer to go with her but she wanted to speak to her dad alone. I'm not sure what Zach would have said but I don't think he would have been unhappy about it. Fliss here wasn't so sure, so said she'd go on ahead and tell him. I waited in the car for her phone call to tell me the outcome. Of course when she told me he was dead and that someone had shot him I scarpered," he admitted offhandedly.

"Why leave?" Andy asked confused. "Surely you wanted to stay and support your new wife?"

"Oh yes," he agreed. "When I got the call I was all for going to the house but Fliss told me to leave. She was quite forceful in fact." He sent her a fond glance. "She thought it would cause trouble especially in light of our marriage. She had wanted to tell Zach before her mother. She knew Jenny was going to be angry, as indeed she was. Then of course all this about the lottery ticket."

"Yes indeed. Now coming to that. Can you explain the circumstances that led to the discovery of the ticket and your confrontation with the deceased?"

Julian let go of Felicity's hand and buried his head in his hands. He stared at the table. "It's been two years since dad died. I've been putting off going through his paperwork but I was at home alone three weeks ago and I just decided to get on with it. I was almost finished, most of it was routine business stuff and of no interest to anyone, when I came across his diary. I flipped through it and between every leaf for that year was a lottery ticket. I was intrigued and went online to see if I could trace any winners. I thought it strange that in the week of his death there was no ticket, so out of curiosity I checked, and lo and behold the winning ticket for the Friday before he died matched all the numbers of all the previous tickets. I couldn't believe it and checked several times but there was no mistake. It was easy then to trace it to Zach even though he left it a month before claiming the winnings. Seventeen million pounds." He shook his head incredulously.

The two women gasped but said nothing. The air in the

room was thick with suspicion, the heat oppressive, yet nobody moved.

Finally Andy broke the silence. "So you went to see Zach. What happened next?"

"It was surreal. I was surprisingly calm even though I'd raced down to Priest's Finger like a madman. I had visions of me ranting and raving like a lunatic, but when I saw him my anger just evaporated. I saw Zach in his study, showed him the diary and all the tickets and we talked like civilised human beings."

Even Andy was confused. "And did Zach deny it? Put up a fight?"

"He didn't do anything. Just sat there behind his desk listening. He said nothing for ages. I remember he shuffled the tickets in his hands and stared into space. I had a feeling he had things on his mind more important than my news. He seemed distracted, then he sort of shook himself out of it. It was then he said would I mind leaving it with him, and to give him a couple of weeks to sort things out."

"What did you say?"

"Well of course I asked him what he was going to do but I got the impression he wasn't too sure. He did say something that confused me a bit though. He muttered something about a doctor's appointment and he'd had some bad news that needed dealing with. I thought he looked ill. He was very pale and I don't think it had to do with my news. It was all very strange."

"And you agreed to wait?" Andy sounded sceptical.

Julian looked up then staring directly at Andy. "I was flummoxed to be honest. Nothing had gone as I expected. I thought we were going to have a violent confrontation and it all fizzled into nothing. I agreed to give him two weeks and then I left."

Nobody spoke for ages. The silence was infiltrated by the distant sounds of cattle in the fields, the far cry of a seagull in flight, the persistent hum of a tractor somewhere near the main road. Suddenly a phone shrilled nearby, making them jump. It was answered immediately, probably by Michael. They heard the phone being put back on its cradle. Silence again.

Andy said introspectively. "So the late Mr Allington had received bad news from his doctor." He looked across the table to Jenny. "Was your husband ill?"

She shook her head. "Not that I know of," she replied indifferently. "We both went to our doctor in London about a month ago. We go private you know. Zach never trusted the local man. Said he was a doddery old sod. It was just a yearly thing. Zach certainly didn't tell me he'd had any bad news and he was a bit of a hypochondriac. A slight cough and he was sure it was deadly. He could never have kept a serious illness to himself."

"You'd better let DS South here have your doctor's name and address before we go. Right, let's get on to you now, Mrs Traversy." He turned to the next page. "Have you got anything to add to your statement?"

She shook her head. "No nothing. I called down to Dad but he didn't answer. I thought he was asleep."

Andy looked at her shrewdly. "You say in your statement that you heard someone coming so you hid in the bushes until they passed? Could you tell if it was a man or a woman?"

"It was just a soft tread like someone tiptoeing yet they must have been in a hurry because they went past quite fast. I was about three feet away hiding behind some yellow gorse. I know it was covered in thorns because I snagged my leg. I had my high heeled shoes on and my feet were killing me as well as my ankle. I waited a couple of minutes, maybe five minutes until I was sure it was clear, then went to the top of the steps. Dad was facing the sea and I don't know if he was dead or alive. He didn't answer either way."

"You didn't see your brother James on the other side of the cove?"

"I didn't see anyone. Of course James is always hiding somewhere. He likes watching people. He's sneaky like that."

105

"So you arrived at the house about twelve, went into the study, then went through the trees, up the hill and along the cliff edge. That would have taken you to about twelve thirty by the time you reached your father."

"I guess so. I walked slower than normal on account of my shoes."

"Do you remember anything else?"

She thought for a moment. She looked tired and drawn. Her brow was furrowed while her fair hair hung damply down to her shoulders. She'd probably jumped out of the shower and into a confrontation with her mother before having a chance to prepare herself for the day's scrutiny. She'd managed to slip into clean clothes though, and gradually as the questioning progressed had a fresh alertness about her. "I do remember a helicopter flying overhead about ten minutes before I got to my father. I think it was hovering out in the bay for a little while and I was just about to leave the bushes when it flew overhead and went away. It was very loud." She shook her head. "That's all I'm afraid."

If what Felicity was saying was the truth then in all likelihood that was the moment the gun was fired. Very opportune for the killer, he thought. He suddenly switched his attention to her mother. Her gaze had barely left the couple since they'd sat down. She jumped visibly. "Okay. Now, Mrs Allington. Let's go over your movements once again. You say you went into the cove at what time?"

Jennifer gave him a fierce look. Tendrils of fine hair had escaped from their glittery clip and glued themselves to the side of her face. She looked less poised than she did on her entrance into the room. He could see a trickle of perspiration make its way slowly down towards her cleavage. She glared resentfully at her daughter and Julian. Obviously, now that the couple had finished she wanted them to leave but they remained seated, waiting for her to speak.

"My statement remains unchanged, Detective. I also wanted to speak to my husband. There was a lot to do and much as I know that my… Zach didn't welcome any intrusions whilst he was in the cove, I felt he had left me no choice but to pursue him there."

"Tell me in more detail your movements starting with the time and what you did after the Reverend Peaceful went into the cove."

Jennifer tutted. "I hardly deem this necessary. I had no reason to want my husband dead. I just wanted to change his mind about giving our money away," she protested indignantly.

"Never the less, Mrs Allington," Andy said abruptly, "We'd like to get the timings sorted out. You do want to find your husband's killer don't you?" he goaded.

"Naturally, Chief Inspector," she said snidely. She raised those ice blue eyes to the ceiling as if seeking relief in the swirling patterns that shifted as the sunlight filtered through the swaying voiles. "Let me see. I left the house about eleven thirty I suppose. I went down to the beach and sun bathed for a short while. I'm not really a sun worshipper and burn easily. I prefer to buy my tan." Her voice sounded bored and disinterested. "Anyway, I needed to get out of the house for some 'me time'. I'd sent Elsa off to Weymouth to get some last bits for the party and decided to get some peace and quiet. Eventually the heat got to me so I went and sat in the shade. I knew I'd have to speak to Zach but thought I'd give him another half an hour lording it over his bit of land. I was about to go into his cove when I heard Ian coming through the trees. I remember that it was just after twelve because I checked my watch. Time was moving on and it was urgent that I speak to Zach before he came back to the house." She laughed bitterly. "Zach wanted the party, but he expected me to arrange everything. He would have come back to the house and shut himself in the study until the last moment. However, Ian dithered on the beach, contemplating God or something, and it was about five minutes before he walked between the rocks and into the cove."

"Did you hear him talking?"

"Oh no. Definitely not. The cove is practically

soundproofed. Any way I gave him about ten minutes then I walked across. Zach was asleep in his deckchair and there was no sign of Ian."

"So why didn't you wake your husband up? It was surely your intention to do so," Andy asked.

"I don't know, Chief Inspector. I guess I just realised that Zach would probably be very angry and start shouting. He was a very stubborn man. There was little or no chance that I could persuade him to change his mind about giving half our money away."

"So you walked away. Did you climb up the cliff on the steps on the right or the left?"

"Neither," she said adamantly. "When the tide is out you can just make it round the bottom of the cliff on the opposite side to the one I entered. There's a few big boulders but it's just about accessible. On the other side there's a grassy slope that's not so steep. It brings you out in the fields by the farm. There's a small worn path that takes you directly to this house. I was indoors when I was told that Zach was dead."

"James came running in?" Andy asked.

She nodded her head and rolled her eyes. "I didn't believe him at first so Fliss and I walked back to the cove. She arrived about the same time as me. He was dead alright. I phoned the ambulance from my mobile and then we waited. Michael turned up a bit later followed by Ian. James was wandering around the cove. He shouldn't have been there. Zach had told him often enough."

"What about this remark of your husband before he died? Your stepson James says that the deceased said it was 'his call'. Any idea what he meant?"

Jennifer gave a bitter laugh. "I expect God did it." She shuddered expressively. "Zach had found religion overnight. He'd called it his epiphany. Wanted to give our money away and throw a party to celebrate the fact. He'd obviously had some sort of mental derangement."

Andy mused thoughtfully. "And you can offer no other

explanation?" he asked.

The three people round the table all shook their heads. "I haven't got a clue," said Julian. "It certainly wasn't what I expected."

"You can't believe anything James tells you, Detective. You may have noticed that he's not all there," Jenny said brutally.

"He seems adamant that his father uttered those words, Mrs Allington."

"To be honest, my brother can be quite malicious sometimes. Him and my father were quite close. He may have made it up. It's the sort of thing he would do," Felicity said candidly.

Andy denied it with a shake of his head. "We find that highly unlikely. Before he died he said it was 'his call'. It must mean something and we would appreciate your thoughts on this. If you have anything to add please inform us as soon as possible."

"I have something to say that may have some bearing but I want to speak in private," Felicity said suddenly.

Julian gave her a frantic look and Jenny eyed her suspiciously. "You'd better say in front of us all, Fliss," her Mother said forcefully. "After all it's at times like this that families should stick together." She gave Julian a malicious look. "Haven't you got things to do?" she said pointedly.

"You seem to forget, Jenny. I'm family now," Julian argued.

"Not in my eyes," Jenny responded bitterly. "You married Fliss under false pretences and as far as I'm concerned, I'm the one responsible for her well-being."

"The only thing you're worried about is the money," Julian shot back. "She's my wife now, so I'm the one who's staying here."

"Oh stop it the pair of you. I'm not a child. I want to speak to the detectives in private so why don't you both leave the room and find something to do," Fliss shouted.

Julian put his arm round her shoulder. "Are you sure,

darling? You know you can say anything in front of me."

Fliss shook her head determinedly. "Yes. I'm sure. This is something I have to do. Neither of you has anything to be worried about, so why don't you both go and let me get on with it."

Julian and Jenny rose from the table and left the room with great reluctance. Jenny looked like she wanted to argue the point, but after one look at her daughter's stubborn face, she left the room.

When it was just the three of them remaining, Fliss drooped over the table and rubbed her eyes tiredly. She looked drained and reluctant to speak, now that she was alone with the two men. Finally, she took a deep breath and raised her eyes. She leant back in the chair and rested her hands on the glass. "I suppose I'd better come out with it. What I'm about to say is a secret that only I know. I don't think it has any bearing on my dad's death and if it hasn't, then I'd rather what I'm about to say stays in this room."

Bill looked at Andy. "I'm not sure we can guarantee that. If it has nothing to do with the case then we will keep it to ourselves."

"I suppose it's as much as I can expect." She took another deep breath. "Here goes. My father was having an affair." She burst out. She looked at the two men expectantly. Neither seemed moved by her confession. It gave her confidence to carry on. "I was in the garden one night, oh, about three months ago. I couldn't sleep so thought I'd get some fresh air. I saw Dad cross the garden. He looked furtive like, so I followed him. He went down to the beach and walked to the centre. He stood there for ages, staring down at the pebbles. There was something there, but I couldn't make it out. Not at first anyway. Suddenly, he began taking off his clothes, until he was naked, standing there in all his glory." She shuddered. "Totally and utterly naked. I couldn't believe it. All that skin. All that flab. At first I thought he was alone and just doing a bit of skinny dipping, then I began to recognise the shape lying on the beach. It was a woman. She was naked too. Lying there. Spread-eagled. I couldn't see her face because she was laying with her feet towards the beach. It was just the top of her head I could make out. It was quite dark, although the moon was out." She paused and shook her head. Her face screwed up in disgust. "They had sex," she finished bluntly.

Andy watched her thoughtfully. "Could the woman have been your mother?"

"Good God. No," Fliss denied emphatically. "They haven't slept together for years. Besides, my mother would never sully herself like that."

"A lot of couples do things that their children would be horrified to know," Andy asserted.

"It definitely wasn't her. This woman, whoever she was, had darkish hair. That much I noticed. She looked bigger as well."

Andy sighed. "And you definitely noticed nothing else about her?"

"I didn't stay around long enough to get acquainted with her," she said sarcastically. "The minute Dad lay on top of her I shot away. It's not the sort of sight you'd expect to see, especially your own father. They looked like a pair of beached whales."

Andy rubbed his hand over his chin. "Okay, Mrs Traversy. We'll have to look into this and try to find the identity of the woman. Just one more thing though. Do you think your mother had any suspicions about her husband's infidelity?"

Fliss gave a cynical laugh. "My mother notices nothing but herself."

Chapter Eight

The old woman that answered the door had an air of gentility about her. She barely reached up to the two constables' shoulders as she ushered them through the dark narrow passageway to the back of the house and into a small, low-ceilinged room. A large sideboard dominated the wall under the window and was choked with useless ornaments which Barton's wife Ellie, referred to as dust collectors. The small paned window was shrouded in thick, off-white nets which blocked out the sunlight and lent a shadowy gloom over the room. Either side of the open fire place sat two old fashioned stuffed chairs, their once vibrant colours muted by time and several layers of grime. In the thin shaft of sunlight which managed to penetrate the murkiness, tiny dust particles floated in its beam. The air was thick and stale and the room had the dimness of a foggy autumn morning.

Miss Battersby sat down. They both watched as the frail body bent to accommodate the shape of the seat, both of them noting that the old, thin bones, so obviously brittle, creaked and groaned in protest. They sounded like they could snap and break at any moment. Collins winced as the old lady shifted with agonising slowness, until finally relaxing against the overstuffed cushion.

"Please sit down, gentlemen, or at least one of you. I'm sorry, I don't normally have any visitors," she croaked sadly. Her voice was low and reedy and they both strained their ears.

Barton remained standing by the door whilst Collins sat in the chair opposite. He lowered himself gingerly. He was a strapping lad and regularly went to the gym. Invalided out of the army in his early twenties he'd built himself up into fifteen stone of solid muscle. His weight boded ill for the fragile chair and especially for the four, six-inch spiny legs that supported the frame. He perched himself on the edge, his knees bent almost to his chest. He speared a telling glance at his partner who was leaning comfortably against the door frame. The latter smiled benignly.

"Miss Battersby," began Collins gently. "Would you mind going over your statement from yesterday please? We just need to clarify a few points."

"Oh I don't mind at all, officer. Though I'm not sure I can add anything to it," she said breathlessly.

"Not to worry," Collins reassured her. He consulted his notebook. "You say you were up by Badgers Wood about twelve fifteen? Is that correct?"

Her head bobbed delicately. "It must have been about that time. I don't have a watch. At my age, time has a habit of dragging along at the slowest pace. The sun was directly over me though, and I left here about eleven or thereabouts. I walk slowly now you know, and I stop frequently."

Collins scribbled in his notebook. "So you can confirm that you saw James Allington walking along the path by the woods at about that time?"

"Definitely. Do you know what, officer? When you get as old as I am, you can afford to be honest. I don't like that young man. Just like his father he is," she confided.

"How come you know the deceased so well?" Collins inquired. The atmosphere in the room was oppressive, like sitting under a heavy, rain laden cloud and a mephitic stench gradually permeated the small enclosed space. Collins screwed his nose against the overpowering smell. The old lady, seemingly unaware of putrid stink, showed only her profile as she stared with pale tired eyes into the open grate. The skin around the skull and face was paper thin, an outbreak of brown liver spots under saggy eyelids, the hair white and sparse. Was this what God's waiting room is like, he wondered disconsolately. He suddenly felt deeply sorry for the old dear, sat there in her upright chair, in this cheerless room, waiting to die. She was quiet for so long but before Collins could prompt her, she spoke softly.

"I was a teacher at the same school he attended in Hammersmith. It wasn't a particularly nice school, lots of

113

poor and dysfunctional children. Zach came into my orbit in his first year. There was something evasive about him. It was like an aura that surrounded him. You couldn't help but feel repelled just being in the same room as him. He had one of those shifty faces and if you don't know what I mean, you only have to look at his son James. Same disposition, same duplicitous attitude."

Silence again while she travelled back to the past. She carried on in a distant almost dreamy voice. "I was a grown woman then. Strong, confident but still quite impressionable, you might say. I'd had a sheltered upbringing you see. Never even dated a man, though I was told on numerous occasions that I was quite pretty. And then, surprisingly, I fell in love. With a pupil in the fifth year," she confessed. She smiled a secret smile from thin colourless lips. "She was beautiful," she admitted shockingly. "Her name was Alice. Alice Jacobs. She had the longest hair, the most flawless complexion and the sweetest nature. Our feelings confused us both. I was completely smitten." She moved her fragile head from side to side.

"Of course it was totally wrong of me. I should have buried my feelings. I had no idea until the moment I saw her, that I was that way inclined." She faced Collins who sat bolt upright in the chair. "Are you shocked?" she asked with a sad smile then closed her eyes briefly. "Of course you're not. It's perfectly acceptable to be a lesbian nowadays, but then…" she sighed. "Then it was completely taboo. My feelings were startling and I was traumatized for months. The very idea was scandalous and totally unspeakable."

"And Zach Allington found out somehow I presume?" Collins asked gently.

She nodded sorrowfully. "I'm not sure how, but I suspect he'd been snooping in my desk. There was a note. I'd written it on the spur of the moment. I think I was disturbed in the classroom and shoved in the back of the top drawer in my desk. He must have read it and drawn his own conclusion. Fortunately, I hadn't mentioned Alice by name in the letter, so she remained out of harm's way, thank goodness. Too late though. The damage had been done. Zach started taunting me, threatening to inform the head teacher. It was the death knell for me and I stopped all contact with Alice."

Collins thought he saw a tiny tear trickle down her cheek. "What happened next?"

They felt rather than saw her shrug. "He left school, I carried on with my life but I had a sad and lonely existence after that. He'd spoilt everything for me you see. After he left I was too afraid to explore my feelings, so I remained unattached and buried myself in my work." She paused thoughtfully. "I never forgot though. Never a day has passed when I haven't regretted the day Zach Allington and I crossed paths."

"And then he came to Priest's Finger?" he said sympathetically.

"And then he came here," she repeated.

"And the torment began again?" Collins said compassionately.

"It was such a shocking invasion of my privacy. He never said anything but it was there in his eyes. Money is never enough for the likes of Zach. They need power as well, and he had that in droves. It was subtle at first." Her voice trembled. "Just the odd sly innuendo and then I was sure he sent James out to watch me." Her head began shaking, her face lowered to her lap. The thin skeleton-like hands gripped liked talons on her bony knees. She breathed her nightmare. "I couldn't leave the house without those prying eyes watching my every move. And then about eight months ago, Zach sent me a letter from his solicitors, putting in an offer for my home. He wanted to kick me out of this house. I nearly gave in but I'm so old and so very tired. Where would I go?" she whispered wearily.

Collins was lost for words. She sounded so defeated, so alone. She began speaking again, her voice so low he could taste her sorrow. It was a strain to hear the words. "And then I got that stupid invitation and I knew then that I would have to kill him."

The two men jumped and looked at each other. Finally, after an age of stunned silence Barton said from the doorway. "But you didn't did you?" he stated, his voice low and emotionless. "We know you couldn't have got down to the cliffs in the timescale. And besides, how did you get hold of the gun?"

"Gun?" she snorted derisively. It took a lot of effort and she breathed harshly then confessed apathetically. "I wasn't going to shoot him. I was going to poison the vermin at his so called revelation party."

Barton moved over to stand behind her chair. "Poison?" he prompted.

"Yes," she said defiantly. "I've been cultivating poisonous mushrooms, death cap actually, for a number of years," she added proudly. "They may look innocuous but they're deadly." She gave her statement in such a matter-of-fact way that you couldn't disbelieve her.

"They say that charity can cover a multitude of sins," Adam mused thoughtfully as he negotiated his car down the narrow lane leading to Priest's Finger. "I mean look at Zach. Was his decision to give away a large fortune an act of benevolence, a sort of gesture of goodwill or was there some ulterior motive?"

Eve looked out of the window, her gaze sweeping over the woodland and vast rolling fields of dry grass. As the car swept round the sharp curve, scattered rooftops appeared, first Miss Battersby's tumbledown thatch, after years of neglect, covered in a dirty brown and green moss. Next door, peaking through the trees the sharp contours of the Peacefuls' roof with its three red brick chimneys. As the view opened up, more house tops appeared then the imposing cream square of Priest's Finger Manor, with its turreted surround, a stark shape against a deep blue background. The sea glimmered on the horizon and several ships skimmed the border between water and the azure skyline. With the window down she could hear the flirting call of wild birds fluttering on the branches of the trees and the lowing of farm animals. It was a peaceful and beautiful scene with a countryside scent that carried across the landscape. Eve sighed and answered. "I think there must have been an ulterior motive. If what Julian says is true then he had no right to give that money away. It was Clive's money wasn't it?" she defended.

"Your money now, Eve. I agree that he had no right to part with that money except to you of course," Adam stated. He pulled over into a lay-by to let the Reverend Peaceful pass in his black Volvo. Muriel sat beside him staring stonily ahead. Neither of them acknowledged Adam or Eve.

Eve turned to look at him. They'd had a wonderful few hours and had talked a lot, but managed to refrain from talking about the murder. Now, being only five minutes from the manor they could avoid it no longer. "I don't want to go back there, not to that house. It holds no happy memories for me and I'm sure Jenny's going to hate me being there," she murmured.

"What Zach did was unpardonable, Eve, but you need to speak to Julian. You need to hear his side of the story," Adam urged.

"What if he killed Zach?" she burst out.

"Do you believe that?" Adam asked quietly.

Eve sighed deeply and shook her head. "Of course not," she answered positively. "But I can say that, can't I? I'm his mother and I know my son. He's no murderer," she asserted. "But what if the police arrest him anyway? He had means, motive and opportunity and isn't that what the police always look out for?"

"Yes it is," he replied honestly, "but I was a cop for thirty-five years and we never arrested anyone until we had absolute proof. Besides," he squeezed her hand and unfurled her fingers, "I know my son. Andy's a good copper and with Bill at his side, he will soon get to the truth."

Eve smiled. "And what about us?" she ventured. "Will we

be helping them with their inquiries? Are we going to seek the truth?"

Adam positively beamed. For the first time in many years he felt a new purpose in his life. A reason to get up in the morning and face a new day. "Damn right we are," he said gleefully. He released the handbrake and the car moved slowly down the hill. "Where shall we start?" he asked.

"What are you asking me for?" she laughed. "You're the one with all the experience."

"Okay," he conceded. "Let's see. If I drop you off at the manor and leave you to speak to Julian I'll go back to the cottage and sort out dinner for tonight. As soon as you're ready give me a ring and I'll pick you up. We'll make some notes and make a game plan."

By this time they'd driven through the gates and Adam pulled to a stop on the gravelled drive outside the front of the house. Eve quickly got out and with a reluctant goodbye, and a promise to ring, made her way round the side of the house to the back entrance. She pushed the heavy door open hesitantly and stepped into the cool hallway. Julian was coming down the curved stairway and she acknowledged him with a wary smile. He stopped on the bottom step and eyed her quizzically. He held up his hands in mock surrender. "Okay before you say anything, I'm sorry."

Eve breathed deeply. Where to begin, she wondered. First things first. Somewhere private where they could speak undisturbed, away from prying ears. She walked over to the door on the left on the other side of the staircase. She heard muted voices in the back lounge and opened the door quietly indicating with a nod of her head for her son to follow. They stepped into a long, narrow hallway in which three doors opened into other living accommodation, including a library that was rarely used. Eve had often sought solace in the gloomy book lined room, and shutting the door behind her ushered Julian to one of the high backed leather chairs that face a bookshelf. She sat in one of the other chairs and faced him. "I've often wondered over the past couple of years whether I could have dealt with your father's death in a different way," she began hesitantly.

"Like how?" Julian interrupted with a challenging glint in his eyes. "You never believed Dad killed himself did you?" he snapped. "But did you do anything about it? Did you push the police to look deeper? No," he accused. "You just sat back and let it all wash over you."

Eve was stunned. She hadn't expected such an angry verbal attack. "No," she protested shaking her head. "It wasn't like that at all. Yes I couldn't believe it but there seemed to be no other option. Your father told us all he was going out for some fresh air. I thought we were all in the house. How was I to know that Zach slipped out after him and pushed him off the cliff?"

Julian buried his head in his hands. "Didn't you wonder why?"

Eve reached over and gripped his arm. "Look at me, Julian. Please," she pleaded when he failed to respond. He lifted his head slowly and mother and son faced each other frankly for the first time in a long while. "I wondered why," she responded adamantly. She looked into dark eyes so like her own and on to a face so like his father's. Blond hair with the same rogue tress that curled over one brow. Fair skin on a round face and a broad Traversy nose that stretched down the generations. Maybe Clive's face had a more leaner look to it, but that could have been brought on by the stress of money worries. Julian was certainly a young version of his father and that still had the power to hurt her. She spoke with her heart. "Every day I've wondered, but in the end I just had to accept that money problems had pushed him over the edge."

"What I don't understand is why didn't Dad tell you straight away about winning the lottery? He must have known? He must have told Zach? Why not you?" he challenged.

She shook her head sadly. She had wondered that herself, but could never come up with an explanation. "I don't know.

Just like I don't know why you didn't tell me about finding Dad's tickets, speaking to Zach and more importantly about you and Fliss," she answered sadly.

Julian flushed guiltily and looked away. "I've been seeing Fliss for about a year and then when she moved to London we got to know each other better. I told her my suspicions about Zach and she believed me," he explained. "We married a few days before I confronted Zach. It was a quick do in the registry office. Both of us felt that in light of all this it might be best to present a united front. Neither of us thought it was going to be a happy family celebration," he finished bitterly.

"I would like to have been there," Eve mumbled. "My only son."

"I'm sorry, Mum," he said sincerely. "I hardly expected to get married myself that way but with every else going on…" he shrugged.

Eve squeezed his arm. This wasn't the time for recrimination. There were more important matters to broach. "Do the police suspect you of murder?" she asked bluntly, staring into his eyes.

Julian squeezed his eyes shut. "I don't know," he answered morosely. "I didn't do it though," he retorted fiercely. "I never went near the house until after he was dead. Fliss phoned me on my mobile and told me to get out of the way. I went to Weymouth and wandered around the town then came back down here about eight o'clock. By then the police were long gone. When we told Jennifer she was absolutely livid. We'd been arguing for hours before you arrived."

Eve shuddered. "I can believe that. Jenny was still screaming and shouting when I got there. She was seething when I entered the room." She shook the memory away and carried on calmly. "Now go over again what happened when you realised Zach had stolen the ticket. Start from the beginning."

So Julian reiterated everything he had said to Andy that

morning. Eve listened carefully.

She'd have to go over it again with Adam later on and wanted a clear and concise account. When he had finished they both sat quietly. Finally she said, "Did Zach seem ill to you?"

"Not really, but then it could have been cancer or something. You can't always tell with that can you? I definitely had the impression that something bad had occurred before I tackled him."

"He didn't look guilty or upset? Think carefully, Julian. You'd just accused Zach of murder and stealing the lottery ticket. Surely there must have been some reaction?" she asked.

Julian shook his head and raked his fingers through his hair. He wore a bewildered expression. "I couldn't believe it either, Mum. He just sat there behind his desk and calmly asked if I would mind waiting a couple of weeks."

"And you just accepted that?" she exclaimed.

"What could I do? I'd run out of steam and Zach seemed to take it so well. He handed me back Dad's diary and the other lottery tickets and slumped back in his chair. I took them and walked out."

"And that's it?"

"That's it."

"So what did you think when you got the invitation?"

"I just assumed by its heading 'revelation party' that he was going to confess or something."

Eve delved into her handbag and brought out the note that Zach had sent her. She handed it over and Julian read it. When he'd finished he turned to her. His face was eager. "So he was going to confess?" he said.

"Well it certainly looks like it."

"What are we going to do now?" he asked. There was a little boy lost about him turning to his mother for help.

She shook her head. "I don't know at the moment but I'm going to talk to Adam. That's Detective Chief Inspector Fortune's father. He's a really lovely man. I met him

121

yesterday and I'm seeing him later."

Her son looked interested. "A new man, Mum?" he quizzed.

Eve blushed. "I only met him yesterday but I like him. Whether it goes anywhere…" she shrugged. "Who knows but I haven't met anyone I've liked enough since your father died, so I'm taking it nice and slow and we'll see what happens."

There was a gentle knock on the door. Julian got up and opened the door. Fliss stood on the threshold looking shy and nervous. She eyed Eve warily. Time to take the bull by the horns, Eve thought, getting up and watching her son guide his new wife across the room. She held out her arms. "We're a small family, Fliss, but I'd like to welcome you into it. I've always wanted a daughter."

Fliss walked into them. She sighed with relief. "Thank you," she said shyly. She glanced towards her husband. Eve saw the look that passed between them, noted the possessive look Julian bestowed on Fliss. They were in love it was plain to see, and Eve was thankful for that at least. She hoped it would be enough to guide them through the turmoil ahead.

Eve invited Fliss to sit and watched her new daughter-in-law. She hoped to God that she didn't turn out like her mother, but only time would tell. Maybe Julian could take her away from all this when it was over. It would be a good idea to part her from her mother's influence, set up a new home as far away as possible. Or maybe they'd want to settle here, she considered. That would put Jenny's nose out of joint but then, she'd surely not want to stay in this house with her daughter and son-in-law. Jenny was a free spirit and Eve could see her jetting off to another country, quite possibly seeking out a new rich husband. She certainly wouldn't waste time mourning Zach. And in light of recent revelations Eve could hardly blame her. Eve didn't like the woman but this could mean a whole new life for her and not necessarily a good one when you couldn't rely on access to someone else's money.

She brought herself back to the present. "Have you spoken to the police today, Fliss?"

"Yes I have. They spoke to us all together except for James and Mike. They say that they don't think James did it and I'm inclined to believe them. James is a bit dim you know."

Eve agreed. "So who do they suspect? Did they say?"

"Well," Fliss said carefully. "There's me and Julian for a start. Mum and Mike. Mr and Mrs Peaceful. Miss Battersby, and Mr Crouch the farmer.

"Oh," was all Eve could say. She frowned. "Can you go over your statement for me, Fliss? What did you do when you arrived at the house and found no one there?"

So Fliss slowly and precisely traced her movements. Eve listened attentively. "So it boils down to this. You arrived about twelve, let yourself into the house went through the study and out into the garden through the patio doors. Did you look in the gun cabinet on your way through?" Fliss said no to this with a shake of her head so Eve continued. "Then you walked the cliff path until you heard someone coming and hid behind a bush. This took you about twenty-five minutes in all. When you were sure it was all clear you carried on and arrived at the top of Funnel Cove about twelve thirty. You called out to your father and received no answer. From what I can gather from the police, your father was still alive and if he'd just been shot, you must have missed the killer by minutes."

Fliss shuddered delicately. "I didn't hear a thing except for some seagulls. There was a helicopter close by but by the time I got to the cliff top it had moved away. When I untangled myself out of the bushes I looked around, but couldn't see anyone near me."

"The trouble with the timings is that it still puts you in the frame, Fliss," Eve said honestly. "They haven't got a precise time for the shot being fired. I gather that your father remained semi-conscious for a while, he even managed to say a last few words, though their meaning is still a bit of an enigma at the moment."

"I understand that, although I can't see why Miss Battersby or the farmer would have done it, so really that leaves six of us in the picture, not eight. It must have been one of us," she said simply.

Eve gasped. The narrowing down of suspects put her son high in the frame for murder. This was bad news. She knew from the discussion last night that none of them had alibis. They were all there in the right area, at the right time. She wondered how the murderer managed to get away unseen. Was it a spur of the moment, unpremeditated murder, or a killing calculated with precision? Eve didn't know but she could feel the net closing in.

"So if what Fliss says is right," Julian ventured, "and I happen to agree, then we're in deep sh…"

"Julian. Language please," Eve interrupted.

He laughed and Eve frowned at him. "This is serious, son. If the police don't find the murderer then a cloud of suspicion will hang over you for the rest of your lives. It's alright here at the moment, we're all cocooned in this house, but when the papers get hold of it, your friends and colleagues will read of it, and then they will be watching you, suspecting you. People have a nasty habit of believing what they want to believe and what if you have children? Can you imagine what will happen?",

Julian sobered immediately and rested his hand on his wife's shoulder. "Sorry," he apologised. "I just need you to believe that neither Fliss nor I had anything to do with it. I trust her implicitly, and strangely enough I trust Zach. I think he was going to say something last night. I think he was ready to confess all and hand the money back to us."

"You think he was going to admit to murdering your father?" Eve asked in disbelief.

Fliss jumped up. "No," she cried. "I can't imagine Daddy doing such a thing. Oh I know he was a bit of a jerk, a thief even, but a murderer?" She shook her head displacing the band in her hair. She brushed the loose strands of hair with her hand. She was shaking visibly and her face was white. "There has to be another explanation," she burst out.

Eve held up her hands and spoke in a placatory tone. "Alright, Fliss. Alright. Now, just supposing you are right. Let me think about it."

"What other explanation can there be?" Julian said regretfully.

Eve thought hard. "Well, what if Zach stole the ticket earlier in the day? As you have already observed, Julian, your father must have told him before he went out of the house that night. Maybe, and I'm only suggesting this for the moment, maybe there was another reason your father jumped off the cliff. Perhaps he didn't jump. Maybe it was an accident. It may be that he went too close to the edge and slipped."

Julian was shaking his head. "You forget. Dad hated heights. He would never have been that careless."

"Your dad had been acting strangely for weeks before he died, sweetheart. I couldn't get through to him. He was depressed about the business. There could have been other things on his mind." She smiled sadly. "Something was worrying him, Julian and I don't know what it was. I don't suppose I will ever know," she concluded.

A look of scepticism passed between mother and son over Felicity's head. For the moment they would leave it at that. Eve gave the young girl a comforting hug, kissed her son on the cheek and left the couple alone. For the moment there were no more words left to say.

Eve stood outside the lounge door, breathed deeply and braced herself. It would be so easy to slip out the house and avoid a direct confrontation with the rest of the family, but if she wanted to protect her son she had to find the real killer. She had no idea how she was going to approach the subject of Zach's death, not in an investigative way anyway. With Jenny's animosity towards her she was liable to fall flat on her face.

Still. She took a deep breath and slowly turned the knob and entered the sunny room. For a short moment she was able to observe the occupants unseen. Jenny sat in one of the chairs facing the patio door. She had her eyes closed and her arms dangled over the sides of the seat. Her brown legs were outstretched. She looked cool and relaxed, her face composed into a mask of sublime peace. Michael had his back to the room staring out of the patio windows and James sat on the opposite side of the room rocking in the chair. James was the first to notice her standing uncertainly on the threshold. The rocking stopped, his small beady eyes stared inquisitively. Never a man for words you nevertheless felt that he was sucking a great deal of knowledge about you with one penetrating look. Zach used to do the same. Getting your measure, gleaning information from your posture, your eyes, your hands. An all-encompassing look that stripped you bare, left you feeling exposed and vulnerable.

Suddenly, as if sensing her presence, Jenny's eyes opened. She gave Eve a cold stare. "Oh it's you," she observed insolently. She looked Eve up and down slowly, taking in every detail. "You look sweaty," she added rudely.

Eve flushed. She'd known this was going to be difficult, should have remembered how much Jenny resented her, and to make matters worse, she was sweaty, could feel her T-shirt clinging to her skin. She smoothed her hand over her hair. It was damp and her fringe felt like it had cemented itself to her forehead. Needless to say, Jenny's hair looked immaculate and immune to the stifling heat. Schooling her face she deliberately closed the door and sat herself down on the centre of the sofa, refusing to be browbeaten, even though she felt like turning and slinking out of the room. She discreetly adjusted her shorts which felt as if the heat was shrinking them and cutting off the circulation in her legs. Michael turned around at his mother's voice. He mimicked his mother's insolent stare. The simmering hate was palpable as her eyes flicked to the mother and her stepsons. For the first time they presented a united front against the interloper who had invaded their family space.

They were waiting for her to speak and she began hesitantly. "I thought I'd pop in to see how you all are coping. I've just spoken to Fliss and Julian," she explained.

"How nice," Jenny said snidely. "And how are the married couple? Still loved up?" she added sarcastically.

"They seem very happy," Eve defended.

"Well of course they are," Michael said bitterly. "Julian's got everything, and Felicity?" he spat her name spitefully. "Felicity has lost nothing." He turned his back on the room again. "It wouldn't surprise me if one of them shot Dad," he muttered under his breath.

"Don't be ridiculous," Eve said forcibly. "Julian had no reason to want Zach dead. They'd already come to an agreement. I'm sure Zach was going to make things right at the party. Someone else wanted your father dead and I'm going to find out who," she revealed recklessly.

Jenny gave a harsh laugh. "You?" she sneered. "What can you do?"

Even Mike laughed at that comment. "What? You think that Dad was going to bring your husband back to life?" he said hurtfully. "Stand up in front of everyone and say 'hey I'm sorry, Eve I killed your husband but hey-ho let me give you the money I owe you'. And you tell me not to be ridiculous? What a joke."

Eve was stung, admitting that that scenario was highly unlikely. She wanted to protest, say something that would defuse the hostile atmosphere. Three pairs of eyes stared at her malevolently, revelling in her discomfort. She remained calm with difficulty. Taking a deep steadying breath she said, "When you say it like that it does seem a bit preposterous," she admitted. "But you have to remember that there's no proof that my husband was murdered. Maybe he did commit suicide," she shrugged trying to appear at ease. "We'll probably never know, but one thing I'm sure of and that is that Zach was going to make amends. How he was going to do that I've no idea."

"There's no proof that Zach stole that lottery ticket either," Jenny said purposely. "Just because the tickets were in Clive's diary doesn't mean they belonged to him does it? Have you seen the diary? Was it a work diary? Remember, Eve," she said disdainfully, "Zach and Clive shared that book. Who can tell if it wasn't swept away and put with Clive's effects when the office was cleared?" she finished on a triumphant note.

Eve felt as if she'd been punched in the stomach. She hadn't thought of that. Clive had never mentioned buying lottery tickets. What if he hadn't? Could Jenny be speaking the truth? Oh God, she thought. If this was true then Julian's account of his interview with Zach was all wrong. It had to be. She'd have to speak to him again. Shaking her head she rose stiffly to her feet and keeping her eyes lowered she left the room. To see the mocking look on their faces was too much to bear right now, but she would be back, and next time she would bring ammunition in the form of ex-cop Adam Fortune.

Chapter Nine

Eve was so agitated when she left the house that she forgot to ring Adam. He looked surprised to see her so soon but taking one look at her face, ushered her into the small cottage and led her on to the patio in the back garden. He guided her to a lounger and left her there while he went into the kitchen to prepare her a cold drink. When he returned she was still staring ahead towards the trees. She looked stunned and worried, and that concerned him. He passed her a drink. She took it abstractedly.

"What happened?" he asked gently.

So Eve told him. Her voice was low and succinct and she told him everything. He listened carefully without comment and when she had finished and seemed to wilt before his eyes, he urged her to finish her drink, led her out the garden gate and walked her down towards the beach. He recognised her need for peace and quiet and time to assimilate her thoughts. He needed time himself, he admitted. The very idea that it wasn't Eve's husband's lottery ticket changed a lot of his perceptions about the case. It was a tricky one because it was going to be nigh on impossible to prove ownership. He pondered on the situation as it stood for Julian while Eve walked by his side, deep in her own thoughts. If it turned out to be true and the lottery ticket did indeed belong to Zach, then what possible motive would there be for Julian to kill the man? Unless of course by asserting that it was his father's ticket and by conveniently marrying Felicity he'd decided to be greedy and have it all. If that was the case then he had a very strong motive.

At some point, and soon, he would have to speak to him. He had been a good police officer and could generally tell at a glance whether a man was a murderer or not and he hoped and prayed, for Eve's sake, and for his own, that the young man was innocent. He gazed at Eve walking quietly beside him. There was something about her that drew him to her. It was a mystery to him why he felt so attracted to her. She was totally opposite, in looks and personality, to his late wife. For the first time since his wife had left home some twenty years previously, he felt a long forgotten flicker of excitement and whilst he admitted painfully to himself that he had loved his wife, he had always known from the beginning of their married life, that he had never been in love with her. It hadn't been a bad marriage though. They had plodded along sedately enough, each carrying on with their separate lives and coming together over the dinner table. And when she had died it had been like the passing of a distant relative, leaving him detached, and only slightly alone.

Life with Eve, if there was going to be a life, was going to be exciting and involved. Already he felt as if they were a couple. It wasn't just that he thought her beautiful, he liked that intelligence that lurked just below the surface, the way her hair hung limply in the heat, the tiny beads of perspiration on her forehead, all those silly things that could be off-putting but weren't to him. She looked straggly and exhausted, her shoulders hunched with worry, her whole posture defeated. Nevertheless, he thought her wonderful and alive, spirited and open and he was captivated. They would get through this he knew. He would make sure of it. He took her hand, she didn't resist and together they walked down on to the pebbles and gazed out to sea.

Barton and Collins left Miss Battersby's house with a great deal of relief. As they walked into the garden, overgrown with weeds and wild flowers, they took deep breaths to rid themselves of the smell that still stuck in their throats. They saw the Peacefuls in their car passing by the gate and Barton muttered, "Damn," under his breath.

"I suppose we might as well interview the farmer now and come back later," Collins said.

His partner agreed and they made their way to their car parked at the end of the lane. It was now one thirty and the sun still hadn't relinquished its unrelenting heat. Pollen danced in the air causing Barton to sneeze. The air outside felt as stuffy as that small room they had just left, and the smell lingered on their clothes and skin.

"That poor woman," Collins said as he looked back at the dilapidated cottage. Even the air surrounding it was heavy with gloom and despondency.

"I almost feel sorry that she didn't murder Mr Allington," Barton admitted. "I'd rather be in jail than in that house."

Collins nodded and they both got into the car. "Blimey, Matt. Get that air conditioning on, will you."

Percy Crouch was busy in the barn. Milking was over and Ben was leading the cows out to pasture in the top field. The officers parked the car by the farm gate and made their way gingerly across the cow-patted yard. Another stench that was over powering awaited them. A huge collie growled ferociously but fortunately was chained by short links to the boundary wall.

"Mr Crouch!" Barton yelled from the barn doors.

The farmer straightened his back and looked over his shoulder. He made his way slowly towards them, his wellie boots squelching in the dung. When he reached them, he sniffed the air appreciatively and reached out his hand. "Wonderful day, gentlemen," he said, impervious to the heat and the incredible smell.

Collins wrinkled his nose. "Just need to go over your statement, sir," he said. "Perhaps we can go somewhere private."

Percy Crouch looked around. "Can't get more private than this," he said.

Barton pointed to the house. "Indoors if you don't mind, sir. It might be a bit cooler in there." And hopefully will smell better, he muttered under his breath.

Percy shrugged. "As you wish." He led the way and opened the back door, which led straight into a large farm kitchen. Dirty plates littered the sink, and most of the worktops that surrounded the room. "Missus out at the market at the moment," he said excusing the mess. "Now sit down the both of you and let's get this over with. Got a lot of work to get through afore the rain comes."

The two officers looked dubiously out of the window. The sky was so blue its brilliance hurt their eyes. Not a cloud dared to intrude against the sun's objective, which was the destruction of anything that marred its horizon. The farmer laughed. "The rain's coming," he asserted positively. "I can smell it."

The only thing they could smell was cow shit but they didn't doubt the farmer's wisdom. These men of the land were canny creatures, they knew. Barton cleared his throat. It was as dry as the Sahara and his voice was gruff when he spoke. "You say you were up here when the murder happened, sir?"

Percy sat down at the head of the table. "Aye," he affirmed.

"And you say you saw Miss Battersby and James Allington by the woods?"

"Aye I saw them both. I only caught a glimpse of the old woman but that young Allington trespassed my lower field. I saw the sneaky bugger and if I didn't have me hands full, what with the cattle and trying to mend me harvester, I would have got me gun out and shot the bastard. He's been warned any number of times."

Barton looked at the previous written statement. "You've been having a bit of trouble with the victim I see. Care to expand on that?"

Percy Crouch slammed his hands on the table. Cutlery and dishes clattered and a cloud of breadcrumbs flew in the air. "Now look here. That man was a wrong 'un. He wanted my land. Now I was safe enough but my Ben? Now that was a different matter."

"Why was that?" Collins asked cautiously

"'Cause I'd already signed over half the land to him. That's the way of it. Father to son and so on through the generations and that dirty beggar been getting at my boy to sell his portion."

"Could he have done that? Surely your son would have held off?"

"Course he couldn't hold off. He's a bit slow that lad of mine. Not as daft as that other bugger at the house, but my lad's gullible like. Zach and that daughter of his were trying to persuade my lad to sell his land. He wanted to build houses I expect. Build his little empire."

"How were they going to persuade him then?"

"That girl started first. Kept going over to him, chatting him up like. Told my boy he could go to London with 'er. He come home with a computer once. Sat it on the table like. My daft boy couldn't even switch the bloody thing on he's that stupid. I told him to take it back. He can do without gifts like that. I warned that man and his girl to stay away from my lad, but no. Next thing I knows my boy and me gets this letter like, offering us pots of money for the farm and land."

"So what did you think when you got an invite to his party?"

"I didn't think nothing of it. Obviously he was going to put on the pressure like. I expect he had a model or something that he was going to show us. Lots of pretty houses dotted over this land but there was no way he was going to persuade me to sell."

There was silence while the farmer brooded. Collins shuffled in his chair. "So were you and your son going to go to the manor last night?"

The farmer snorted. "Not bloody likely. We got better things to do with our time. Farm work's not a nine to five job, you know. The cattle still need milking and there's plenty to do in the yard. We have to be up at four. Early to bed and early to rise. That's a farmer's life for you."

"Did you kill Zach Allington?" Barton asked bluntly.

Percy shook his head. "I wanted to. Really I did. It crossed my mind many a time," he said defiantly. "But I never got the chance. The bloody harvester broke a spring and it took me ages to fix it. Then it was milking time.

Fortunately for me some other bugger had the privilege."

"How were you going to kill him then?" Collins asked interestedly.

Percy hunched his shoulders. "Dunno really. Hadn't quite made up my mind. I gotta shotgun, some poison and plenty of heavy objects but unluckily for me, no time. Whether I would have done it, given the chance, I can't say but I sort of worked my way up to it. Still," he added philosophically, "somebody's done me a great favour, and I ain't going to be hypocritical and say I'm sorry the man's dead. 'Cause I'm not."

"Do you have any witnesses that saw you at the relevant time?" Barton asked.

Only the missus and the dog. The farm hands had finished and I was up to my ears in it in the barn. It's only by chance that I saw the old lady and that James. I'd popped into the kitchen here for a quick bite to eat."

"You didn't see anyone else then?"

"Nope. Not that I was looking. I only took notice of James 'cause I knew the bugger was going to cross my land. Why he can't walk the cliff path like the rest of them I don't know."

"Can you see the cove from here?" Collins asked.

"Nope. You have to walk down church hill. That takes you right to the edge of the cliffs, then the path follows along to the manor and the other beach."

"Do you remember hearing a helicopter about twelve thirty or thereabouts?"

The farmer shook his head. He was starting to get impatient. He stood up signalling an end to the interview. "Like I said, I was mending the harvester. Had the engine on so couldn't hear a thing. Normally I'd do that kind of job outside but my outdoor power point's not working, so had to clear the barn and cram the machine in there."

The two officers stood up ready to leave. They thanked the farmer and as they approached the door, they heard a car approaching. "That'll be the missus back from market," the farmer explained. "Means I'd better get on with me work. The missus don't like me loitering about, especially in 'er kitchen."

Mrs Crouch proved to be a miniature of her husband. Short and stout with a rugged weathered complexion, pudgy fingers and a flowery pinafore over her portly frame. Heavy Dr Martens and fat spotty legs finished the picture of a hard uncompromising farmer's wife.

She gave them a look, wooden as if sculpted by sandpaper and passed them without comment.

"It no good speaking to 'er," said Percy truculently. "She don't like strangers who ask impertinent questions and she never takes note of the doings of the rest of the folk round here."

Barton and Collins decided to take his word for it and drove away from the farm sure in mind that the farmer, his wife and son had nothing to do with the murder. They joined the main road and made their way back to the station in Abbotswood, their progress hampered by the X53 bus service as it made its way slowly along the windy road, its passengers happy with the journey overlooking the Jurassic coastline.

They were surprised however, on arriving at the police station to see the black Volvo, owned by the Peacefuls. They'd probably decided to conduct their interview within the confines of the station, Barton decided, as he and Collins made their way to the small canteen, avoiding the main offices. Drinks first and a little something to eat.

Andy was not amused when he was informed that the Reverend Peaceful and his wife were in reception, insisting that they wished to see him personally. He had a pile of paperwork in his tray to be addressed, and although the switchboard had diverted many of his calls he felt clogged down with work. He'd given explicit instructions not to be disturbed so his immediate reaction at their imminent arrival to his office was an explosion of anger, especially as he'd already assigned the job of interviewing the Peacefuls to Barton and Collins. He'd deal with them later, he thought muttering an expletive under his breath.

South was busy munching a sad looking sandwich at his desk. His eyes studied the computer screen, his tough-looking hands scrolling the statements. Every now and then he would mutter inaudibly and write something down on his notepad. South was a genius with computers, but still preferred the outdated way, having written statements accompanied by a selection of explanatory notes, which he could keep to hand. His explanation that you couldn't carry a computer around with you was to Andy's mind a valid reason.

"I'll speak to the Reverend in here, South and you take Mrs Peaceful to the interview room," Andy said resignedly.

South straightened his back and swivelled his chair to face Andy. He brushed crumbs from his trousers and stared hard at his boss. "You still mad at me?" he asked boldly.

Andy did his best to keep his face expressionless, but a slight smirk broke on his lips. "Shouting out the window at a cyclist and calling him a psychopath is not on, South, and you know it," he rebuked.

South snorted derisively. "If you'd care to let me explain, sir," he protested. "I did not call the man a psychopath." At Andy's raised eyebrows he explained, "I said cycle path. The idiot was on the road. What's the point of paying out thousands of pounds to keep these people safe when they go on the main road? Bloody annoys me it does."

Andy laughed outright. "My apologies, South. My hearing must be going. I'm sure there's a word for that you know."

"Homonym I think the word is, sir. Something about having a double sense," South intoned. "Not that cycle path is a true homonym. Now 'chicken', that's a good one and 'bark' of course and 'book' and one of the words spelt differently is 'aloud' and 'allowed'. There's hundreds of them," he added smugly.

Andy looked at him bemused but an idea slowly

permeated Andy's mind. "I wonder…?" he reflected. "Do you think that our man's last words might be some sort of homonym? 'His call. His call'. Could he have meant something completely different? Do you know I might get my father on to this. He's a bit of a crossword fanatic. I'll ring him in…" A knock at the door interrupted his musings and Mr and Mrs Peaceful were admitted into the room. Andy nodded to South who quickly stood up and ushered Mrs Peaceful back into the corridor and into a smaller room next door.

Andy immediately apologised. "Sorry about that, Reverend, but I'd prefer to speak to you alone. DS South will look after your wife and go over her statement. Why don't you sit down?"

Ian Peaceful complied but looked annoyed. He sat in the uncomfortable, high backed chair, facing the window. At this time of the afternoon the sun had lost its blazing intensity and the small white washed room sat in the shadow. The room was still stuffy though, the air thick in the sultry heat. The Reverend, dressed in his normal attire of black top and black faded jeans stretched out his long legs and placed his hands on the desk. He had a pietistical look on his face as he stared directly at Andy. Andy in turn straightened his tie then picked up the statement. "I'm surprised to see you here, sir," he began. "I have sent two of my officers to interview you in your home."

Ian Peaceful gave a sanctimonious smile and closed in his hands in benedictal prayer. "An Englishman's home is his castle, Detective Chief Inspector, and I don't like it invaded by our police force," he said self-righteously. "That's why I brought my wife here. The police officers you sent were with Miss Battersby when we left and we do have better things to do with our lives than waiting around for someone to call."

Andy sighed his displeasure but kept his face expressionless. He didn't like the man or his holier than thou attitude. Was this enough to make him a murderer though? Andy wondered. He had met many killers and the Reverend was as glib, and superficially charming as a great many of them. The man showed no sign of discomfort. He sat with his eyes, dark as flint, staring with a forbidding look around the room. Here was a man more likely to be piercing the Lord's flesh with a spear than kneeling in prayer at his feet, Andy thought abstractedly. He shook himself from his reverie and attacked the interview with relish. He was determined to wipe the condescending smile off the smirking lips. He shuffled the papers. "We've been looking into your past and your relationship with the deceased," he began.

The Reverend gave him a furtive look. "I have nothing to hide and I've already admitted to knowing Zach when we were at school together."

"Yes I know, sir, but you failed to admit just how close your relationship was with him," Andy said knowingly.

"I don't know what you mean. Perhaps you'd care to explain," the Reverend replied crossly but his composure had been rattled. He wondered how much they had found out and how much he should confess. His face hardened, tightening the skin on his face. His lips thinned as he struggled to regain his self-assurance. He noted the other man's confident smile. Ian had no compunction about lying about his past; he'd had years of experience doing just that. He was sure his secret had died with Zach, but what if it hadn't? What if others knew? What if Zach had told someone else or left something to incriminate him? "How much do you know?" he burst out.

Andy adopted a confidential tone of voice. "We managed to locate certain individuals that were close associates of you and Zach at your school in Hammersmith. Some have given us some very enlightening information," he disclosed smugly.

Ian bit off an angry retort. He took a sneaky look over his shoulder at the door and turned with a resigned look at Andy. The officer's face was inscrutable and because of it, Ian's condescending attitude withered. He gave a half-hearted laugh. "Rumours? Is that what you call evidence,

DCI Fortune? Wicked hearsay from a few teenage boys?"

"Men now, sir," said Andy briskly, amazed at the astonishing display of cowardice and mendacity of a member of the clergy. "Men with long memories who have signed statements detailing their powers of retention," he added with angry accusation.

Ian felt a pervading sense of menace. He didn't know how long he could last without blurting everything out, confessing and exposing his soul. His shoulders slumped. He gave in with frightening ease. "It was just a one off," he confessed. "I was young and foolish. It wasn't just me," he whined.

"You rented your body out for money, sir," Andy said brutally. "You prostituted yourself with goodness knows how many men. How long did it go on before you stopped?"

Ian shuddered. He was browbeaten. "Just a couple of months," he muttered. "There was a group of us, all from poor families. I thought Zach was one of us, but all along it was him farming us out. He must have been making a fortune because we certainly weren't. Every week Zach would go around and hand out the cash. I just assumed, along with a few others, that Zach was selling his body as well, but I found out, not so long ago that in fact, he was actually our pimp."

"And you killed him because of it?" Andy said mercilessly.

The Reverend jumped up, knocking his chair to the floor. "No!" he shouted. He paced the room like a caged animal, muttering. "I didn't kill him. I went to the cove and he was asleep. I knew he was going to tell everyone at that damn 'revelation party' of his. Can you imagine the scene, the humiliation? Zach Allington, standing on his damned pedestal and proclaiming to all and sundry that I was nothing more than a cheap, tarty rent boy. It would have destroyed me, would have destroyed my marriage. I couldn't stand it. I went down to the cove to make him change his mind but I took one look at him and knew nothing I said would make the slightest difference." He stopped pacing and came back to the desk, standing over Andy and daring him with his eyes to disbelieve him.

Andy remained cool, aloof and imperturbable even though he felt an instinctive sense of imperceptible repugnance against this man. He leant casually back in his chair and watched the Reverend indifferently. "So your wife has no idea about all this?"

"God. No. She doesn't have a clue. It's not something I'm proud of," he declared vigorously.

Andy eyed him with displeasure. "And yet you became a man of the cloth? Why was that?"

Ian Peaceful sagged in resignation. "There were other incidences," he admitted reluctantly. "When I left school I got into debt. I needed money urgently. It was an impulsive, spur of the moment thing and I got caught. My father gave me an ultimatum. He would pay off my debts if I would go into the church. He was a very religious man but could be cruel. He was impervious to my pleas and threatened me with exposure. My friends, family, colleagues, he would have told them all. He left me no choice. The fact I didn't believe in God meant nothing to him."

Andy put his elbows on the desk and folded his hands beneath his chin. If anything the air in the room had become even more oppressive. The scent of crisp, cut grass accompanied by the not so sweet smell of cow manure crept insidiously through the open window. Andy still found it difficult not to miss the delicate aroma of car fumes and diesel that fermented the air in his old office in the centre of London and although the heat in the capital could be totally debilitating, at least his office had good air conditioning. It also sported a well-run, nutritious canteen which served good wholesome food. Which reminded him that he was hungry, not having eaten anything but a slice of dry toast several long hours ago. His stomach gave an answering growl, it could almost taste the limp cheese and onion sandwich which was probably the only item of food on offer. But for now the tension in the room was palpable. He could feel the Reverend's impatience to get out of the office and if he hadn't been in such need for food he would have loved to prolong the interview.

"I think for the moment we will end this interview but if you can confirm one small thing for me? Do you remember a helicopter hovering about the time you were in the cove?" Andy asked.

The Reverend stared into space, scrunching his eyes in thought. "I think there may have been one," he answered vaguely. "I certainly remember the sound of those noisy jet skis farther along the coast and there could have been a helicopter out at sea, but I can't be a hundred per cent sure."

Andy was disappointed. He was sure that the helicopter had masked the sound of the gun being fired and if it had been out at sea then maybe the Reverend hadn't committed the murder. He picked up the phone and instructed the officer at the desk to send someone up to his room and escort Ian Peaceful to the waiting room. "As soon as DS South has finished with your wife I'll have her sent down to you. No doubt we will need to speak to you again but in the meantime if you would inform us if you intend to leave the area." He stood up and walked Ian to the door, opening it and handing him over to Sergeant Harper. "Take the Reverend Peaceful downstairs and give him a drink if he'd like one," he told the officer.

Neither man said goodbye or shook hands. Ian Peaceful looked wretched, a shadow of the man who had entered the room, and he followed the officer docilely along the corridor.

It was only five minutes later that South re-entered the office. "Canteen first," Andy said before the other man could speak.

Another ten minutes later and the two men sat at the Formica table. The remains of spilt sugary drinks had left the surface tacky and both chose to cradle their respective drinks in their hands. Both munched on biscuits, the only available food left in the glass cooling cabinets this late in the afternoon. Both also had mugs of steaming tea and tumblers of iced water. Andy spoke first, from memory reciting the half an hour with the Reverend. South nodded here and there and asked the odd question but seemed benignly immune to the Reverend's confession.

"It doesn't surprise me. I've always found it odd to chain yourself to the church whether you're married or not," was his only remark.

"What about the wife then?" Andy asked. "Anything there?"

South rolled his eyes expressively. "Well, sir. Seems like our staid and respectable wife is nothing short of an adulterer."

"Andy's head shot up. "What? Not her and Zach Allington surely," he exclaimed.

South nodded. "Her and the deceased," he said with relish. "If she's to be believed, her and the victim have been at it like rabbits for months. Apparently." And here he gave a little chuckle. "They were lonely. They'd been indulging in some lonely, hot sex."

Andy was stunned. "Don't be so crude, South." But even he admitted to himself that the thought of the dowdy Lay Minister in the throes of passion with the dead man did take some believing. "Did you believe her?"

"Strangely enough I do. There was something so emotionless when she confessed."

"How long has it been going on? Did her husband know?"

South shook his head. "Her husband wouldn't notice if she ran around naked. He's too self-centred to notice anything unless it involves him, and she admitted as much. She says that the sex stopped about two months ago. Zach stopped calling and the relationship just petered out. I didn't get the impression that the lady was too upset about it," he observed.

"Did she kill him?"

"I'm pretty sure she didn't, sir. Nobody saw her going on to the beach. I get the feeling that if her husband did do the killing that she wouldn't be too upset about it, and if she had followed him into the cove and Zach was dead, she wouldn't have covered for him."

"She could have been his accomplice," Andy stated unconvincingly.

"Nah," South dismissed. "Not a chance. There's not a lot of love between them." He finished his drink and put his mug down. "What about our Reverend then, sir? Did he do it?"

Andy sipped on his drink. His coffee was still hot. South had finished his. South must have a cast iron stomach, he thought. There was just the two of them sitting in the canteen now. They could hear the staff pottering in the kitchen and the sound of clinking glasses and running water. Within the next hour the night staff would be on duty and they only had a short time to collaborate the latest statements. "I'm not so sure about the Reverend. My gut feeling tells me he didn't do the murder. He's a coward, all talk and no action. He sticks firm to his original statement that the deceased was asleep when he entered the cove and that must be so, unless Mrs Allington is lying, and I can't see why she should. There's only one person she cares about and that's herself. Oh, and maybe her daughter."

"I'm inclined to agree with you, sir, but in that case the field of suspects narrows down quite dramatically. It can only be Zach's wife, son, daughter or Julian Traversy. Four of them and each with the same motive. Our victim was hardly going to expose any secrets about his own family, so money it must be. And not one of them can be eliminated."

They got up and left the canteen, making their way once again to the stuffy office. Andy called to Barton and Collins when he passed their room and instructed them to come to him as quickly as possible. This they did with impossible haste. They were nearing the end of their duty and both were eager to get home. The office felt crowded when they all congregated around the desk. Andy went first followed by South. Barton and Collins spoke together, giving their statements. "It's the old woman I feel sorry for," Collins said. "She's got no family or friends. I think she wanted to be immortalized for all time by poisoning Mr Allington. The man ruined her life as I see it. I'm not saying he deserved to die, sir, but it's difficult to feel sorry for him."

"Have we had the coroner's report yet, sir?" Barton asked.

Andy shuffled in his in tray finally pulling out a sheet of paper. He perused it quickly then nodded. "Yes here it is. Just as we thought. The bullet was still in him, lodged behind the left eye. The coroner reckons that Mr Allington may have lived for about fifteen minutes after the shot. He thinks any more is highly unlikely. So the gun was fired about twelve thirty at the latest. This is not set in stone though. Who can tell how the human body will react. If a man can live after being shot in the head he might last longer, maybe even thirty minutes, so I still think we should expand our time by another ten minutes, giving us between twelve fifteen and twelve forty. Remember James Allington was in that cove at twelve forty-five and his father was just about alive then."

"What about the helicopter, sir? We've been on to Portland base. It was one of theirs, out on a practice run. They weren't looking into the cove but they were in that vicinity about twelve thirty which may have been when the gun was fired. Something had to have muffled the noise."

Andy looked up and smiled. "Well done the pair of you. I was going to ask you to look into this helicopter affair but you've pre-empted me. Now before you go, do either of you know what a homonym is?"

Both men looked confused. "No, sir," they said in unison.

"Well I think I'm right when I say it's a word that sounds the same, but has a different meaning." He went on to explain his mistake with South. "So he shouted out of the car window to the cyclist to get on the cycle path. I misheard and thought he was calling the man a psychopath, so I'm thinking that maybe, what our victim whispered on his dying breath was not 'his call' but something very similar." He looked around at the three men. "So what do you think?" he asked.

"Off the top of my head, sir, I can't think of anything that could be mistaken 'his call'," Collins said.

"I can see where you're coming from," Barton said. "I mean when a bloke's lying there dying, he's hardly likely to say 'his call' is he? He might say 'your call' or 'he called' or maybe he said 'histor' and meant history or something or even 'historical'. There could be hundreds of words in the dictionary that could be similar."

Chapter Ten

Jennifer Allington stormed into the room. "Really, Michael, must you slouch like that?" she snapped. She walked over to the patio doors and turned to face the room. She sent a look of dislike at James who was draped untidily over the glass table, his head buried in his arms. She sniffed. "And how many times have I told you not to smoke in the house," she fumed.

Mike grinned insolently. "What's the matter, Jen. We can do what we like now that Dad's dead. It's our house now."

"My house actually," she reminded him. "Where's Fliss?" she asked. "She's not in her room."

"Out with hubby I shouldn't wonder. Probably working out how they're going to spend all the money." He gave his stepmother a sly smile. "I expect they'll sell this place," he said looking around the room.

Jenny glared at him. "Why would they do that? This house and all the money belongs to me now. Nobody can prove that Zach didn't buy the lottery ticket, especially Eve."

"Oh come on. We both know that Dad didn't have a gambling bone in his body," he retorted. "He looked bloody stunned. Couldn't even remember buying the ticket. I always thought it strange."

Jenny speared him a glance of pure hatred. Her eyes flashed. "Didn't stop you spending his money though did it?" she jeered. "You were as ready to accept it as the rest of us."

Mike jumped up. "So what?" he shouted angrily. "We didn't know then that Clive had hundreds of tickets with the same numbers did we? And all that rubbish you spouted to Eve about the diary being the office diary. Crap, the lot of it. You were working in the office then. You would have noticed lottery tickets between the pages. No. We'd better accept the inevitable. Clive won the money, and Dad pushed him over the cliff to get his hands on it." He flung himself back in the chair, the force sending it slamming against the wall.

James jumped and sent a distressed look across the room. He began rocking in his chair. Jennifer eyed him contemptuously. "And you can shut up," she snarled.

"Leave him alone," Michael shouted. "It's hardly his fault is it?"

"Oh brotherly love, Michael," Jenny pronounced each syllable sneeringly. She moved farther into the room and folded her arms. Looking into the mirror she smiled at her image and tilted her head. A few pinpricks of Botox above her eyes and collagen fillers around her upper lip had given her a more youthful appearance. A chemical peel had smoothed out any wrinkles, a chin implant had defined her jawline and pouted lips had enhanced the overall look she'd wanted to achieve. Adding all that with a personal trainer had given her a honed body that matched her face. She tilted her face and stroked her hand across her cheek. What money could buy, she thought to herself. Even her clothes were bought from the best designers. She stepped back from the mirror and looked down to her feet. Immaculately dressed as always; today she wore fitted black leggings, a purple silk top and sandals of the softest leather.

Her eyes caressed her surroundings speculatively. Although Zach had insisted that the main body of the house including his study, hallway, and library were kept in keeping with the history of the house, he'd left the rest to her. The first thing she'd got rid of was the ornate covings and ceiling roses and all the other old fashioned additions to the manor. She furnished an air of ambiance and modern tranquility to their home with expensive touches and up to date furniture. It was pleasing to her eye and added the right touch to proclaim their wealth to their more circumspect visitor, and although she hated living in this backwater, she enjoyed seeing the envy in the eyes of old friends and business acquaintances as they drove up the driveway, to be met by the impressive facade of the manor.

Although she schooled her features into calm acceptance

of the problem facing her, she was in fact deeply worried. Her dream of selling the house and moving to London, tea at the Ritz and shopping in Harrods was hanging in the balance. She was loath to admit it but what Mike had proclaimed was valid. She had a fight on her hands yet she couldn't help but congratulate herself inwardly. Thankfully she'd made a few contingency plans when they had received the lottery money. An agreement with Zach to hide a large quantity of the winnings in a separate account filled her with relief. It was money that couldn't be touched by anyone now but herself. She'd then had the foresight to move the money in dribs and drabs until the bulk had been moved into a secret account in her maiden name. At some time in the near future she'd intended to skip the country for a sunnier climate, and begin a new life without Zach. But now, with Felicity settled with that Traversy boy, and with the danger of her stepsons becoming an incumbent to her, it might be a good idea for her to put those plans into action, now. Today even, she thought.

James meanwhile gave the pair a strange look. He opened his mouth then closed it again. Once again the other two ignored him and his face took on a confused frown. Something niggled on his memory but the harder he thought the more bewildered he became. Should he speak to Fliss, he wondered, or maybe Mike? Yes he decided. He'd speak to Mike. Mike had stopped Jenny being nasty to him. He would help un-muddle the thoughts whirling around his brain. Daddy had spoken to him. He'd told him who killed him, but the words had confused him. Now, suddenly he began to understand. He gave his stepmother and brother one last penetrating look, stood up, and slipped silently out of the room.

The air was cooling now as he trod the well-worn path across the field towards the cove. He was so deep in thought that he ignored the threat of the farmer. He stumbled down the cliff path and rested wearily on the rocks. The tide was high, slapping against the cliff face inches from his feet. He leant back and stared reflectively out to sea. He worriedly chewed his bottom lip and wondered what Daddy had done to get himself killed, and why the person who had made a hole in his head had done it.

Felicity and Julian strolled hand in hand along the coastline. A cool, easterly breeze ruffled her hair as they navigated through the gorse that followed the coastal path. Out on the horizon clouds started to form as the sun began to lower in the sky. They had spent most of the day together, both loath to spend more time than necessary in the manor, but they both knew it was nearly time to go back. They stopped and stared out to sea. Felicity broke the silence. "I've always liked your mother you know," she said reflectively. "And your dad too."

Julian nodded. "My mum's a good person. She wasn't happy about the wedding though. I think she would have liked to have been with us." He turned to her and clasped both her hands looking deep into her eyes. "We're going to be alright you and I," he promised. "My mum will come around, and I know she likes you as well. We'll get through this and when it's all over we can decide whether to keep the manor. I don't mind moving away from here but ultimately it will be your decision. I don't want to live with your mother though, Fliss," he said firmly. "She's never going to accept me and when all this lottery money is sorted out I don't think we will see much of her."

Fliss lowered her eyes sadly. "I just seemed to have lost everybody. Not you of course. We'll always have each other and maybe, one day we'll have children, but to lose Daddy like I did." She shrugged. "I just feel a bit alone I suppose."

He hugged her tightly. "I understand, Fliss. I lost my dad too remember. And those circumstances were horrible as well. Even worse now is wondering whether he fell or was pushed."

Fliss sighed deeply. "I know," she said. She pulled away from his embrace. "Come on. Let's be strong. I have a bad feeling that it's going to get a lot worse before it gets better."

Once again four people sat around a table. Bowls of salad and assorted cheeses adorned the tablecloth. A couple of bottles of Las Falleras Rosé was being passed around, its fruity bouquet teasing the air. It was near seven in the evening and the setting sun sent shards of its brightness through the trees that surrounded the small cottage. Mingling with the aroma of the wine was the subtle scent of the foxgloves and roses, stocks and honeysuckle, that sprayed splashes of colour on the edges of the unkempt garden. A pair of chattering magpies battled in the treetops causing twigs and leaves to fall to the ground. The four people sat on rickety chairs that had seen better days and their conversation was concentrated on the day's respective investigations.

"I don't need to tell you that this conversation is for your ears only, Dad and you too, Eve," Andy said.

Adam quelled him with a telling look. "Naturally, son," and Eve just nodded.

So Andy, with interjections from Bill South, told them everything they had learned throughout the day. "I've half a mind to take the Peacefuls off the list, although that doesn't mean I totally discount the Reverend. He definitely had means, motive and opportunity. And push come to shove, when cornered, he's very likely to strike out and kill. It all balances on Jennifer Allington's statement, that her husband was alive and sleeping when she followed the Reverend into the cove. I can't see her lying to protect him. Why would she? The man's a smouldering volcano though. Just waiting to erupt. Yet there's something. Not quite tangible I admit, that tells me he didn't do it."

"I think I'd kill any man that implied I was some sort of rent boy," South snapped.

Andy looked at the big man by his side and laughed. He patted him on the arm. "I don't think you have any worries in that quarter, Bill," he assured.

Bill huffed. "Should bloody well hope not."

"Anyway. We can definitely rule out Miss Battersby and Farmer Crouch. I also think we can eliminate Muriel Peaceful and James Allington." He looked directly at Eve. The look in her eyes told Andy she knew what was coming. "Unfortunately that leaves your son Julian, his new wife Felicity and Michael and Jennifer Allington. Anyone of them could have done it and each one of them fits the criteria for this crime."

Adam gripped Eve's hand. "Andy's not saying he did it, Eve, but he has to keep Julian in the frame." He looked at her honestly.

"I know it probably won't make things better, but nobody saw your son in the area at the relevant times, and with all the toing and froing that was going on, I'd say it was nigh on impossible for him to slip to the murder scene without being noticed. As Michael Allington explained, it was like Piccadilly Circus on that beach," Andy said reassuringly.

Eve was slightly mollified. "I just can't believe that Julian or Fliss did this terrible thing. And why now? What about anytime in the last two weeks? I spoke to Julian and Fliss this morning and he said he was shocked that Zach had made him wait. I mean, did you find out why Zach went to the doctor for instance? Was he ill, dying or anything? Was it anything to do with this epiphany thing he had?"

Andy shuffled some papers on the table. "Yes. Here we are. The post-mortem results are quite clear. Zach Allington was in reasonably good health. Nothing serious going on with him. Overweight of course, and smoked too much, but nothing life threatening. One of the team got hold of the private clinic that he and his wife went to for their annual check-ups. The doctor they normally see was away on holiday for a month but they spoke to another of the partners who confirmed the post-mortem results, so a dead end there I'm afraid."

"So why mention it to Julian?" Eve asked confused.

Bill and Andy shrugged. "No idea," they said in unison.

"Julian didn't mention anything more about that subject I suppose?" Andy asked hopefully.

Eve shook her head. "No he didn't. Sorry. It's a bit of a mystery isn't it?" She looked to Adam for support. "I spoke to the rest of the family though." She shuddered. "It was a very unpleasant experience." Eve explained the scenario in the lounge. "I can't believe that Clive left all those lottery tickets in the firm's diary. He did have his own private diary, although it's going to be difficult to prove and why didn't Zach tell Julian that if that was the case?"

"It certainly would have been common knowledge if the diary was in the office all the time. No, Eve. I think the family is clutching at straws there," Andy assured.

"But difficult to get it confirmed," Bill interjected.

Adam nodded his head thoughtfully. "Difficult but not impossible. I'm a hundred per cent sure that Eve's husband was the rightful owner of that lottery ticket."

Eve squeezed his hand. "Thank you, Adam," she said and relaxed in the chair. It was such a relief to have someone by her side who believed her.

Adam leaned forward and put his elbows on the table. "Just out of curiosity. Who was in the house when Clive Traversy died?"

Eve answered before Andy had a chance to speak. "Just the seven of us. Michael and James were somewhere else in the house doing their own thing. I remember Fliss flitting in and out but they weren't visible most of the time. Mostly it was the four of us. Me and Clive, and Zack and Jenny."

"Did you have dinner together often?" Adam asked curiously. "Bar your husband and Zach having a business relationship, I can't see that you and Jennifer have much in common."

"Eve grimaced. "It happened more often than I liked, that's for sure. I think it was more Zach and Clive used it as an excuse to get together, talk business and have a few drinks. Jenny and I talked about mundane things. Nothing interesting I can assure you. I think we were both there under sufferance really."

"So," Andy said thoughtfully. "Same old faces then. We'll discount you of course, Eve. Realistically then, Michael and Felicity were in the frame for your husband's death as well. If they were in the house and you only saw them intermittently then, maybe, one of them could have killed Clive as well. That rather discounts Julian though. If Clive Traversy was murdered, then I think the same person must have committed the crime. Two murderers… and in the same family?" He shook his head. "I think it highly unlikely."

"But would they have known about the lottery ticket?" Adam asked.

"That's a valid point but I think again that's unlikely," Andy admitted. "And I can't for the life of me see any other reason for killing Clive."

"They might have noticed something though," Eve said. "I don't remember the police questioning any of them. I suppose it was clear cut to them that Clive had either slipped or jumped off the cliff."

"Make a note of that, Bill. We'll ask them tomorrow."

Bill complied and the four of them sat companionably back and sipped their wine. Andy stretched. "Have you had any thoughts on that little conundrum I set you, Dad?"

"What?"

"His call. Zach's last words. We've been over and over it all day. I've set some of men on to it but I've had no feedback yet."

"Do you suppose it was part of a sentence maybe?" Eve asked.

Andy shrugged. "Who knows, but I'm sure if we can find the answer to it, we might find our killer."

Just then South's mobile screeched its tune into the silence. South spoke brusquely. "Yes. What is it?" He listened intently. "What do you mean, who is it? What? Your bloody mentor of course. Now what do you want?" More silence from Bill. "DCI Fortune is busy right now. Can't you give me the message? No. Right." Bill put his hand over the mobile.

"That fool Townsend, sir. Wants to speak to you. He sounds upset."

Andy rolled his eyes resignedly and took the phone. "Yes, Nick. What's the problem? What? Don't be daft, man. No he didn't. Well I'm sure I appreciate that, Nick, but DS South did not say you were mental. No. I heard him as well. When you asked who he was, DS South said he was your mentor. Not you're mental. Perhaps you need to get your ears unblocked. Now what was so urgent you had to phone at this time?" Andy pulled a pen from the inside of his jacket that was draped over the back of the chair, and began scribbling furiously. When he had finished he passed the mobile back to South. South was smirking and Adam and Eve hid their smiles behind their hands.

"Another one of them there homonyms, sir," he laughed and went on to explain the mistake of the afternoon that had got Andy angry with him.

When the rest of the party had finished laughing Adam turned to his son. "Important news, son?" he queried.

"Just the details of the Zach's bank account. It seems within a few weeks of banking the lottery win, our dead man started to transfer several millions to another account. Further checks have revealed that said money is no longer in that account and seems to have disappeared."

"Perhaps he spent it all," South observed.

Can't see that he has, South. He had seventeen million in his bank only two years ago. Even taking into the equation the manor house, cars and a wife like Jenny." He shook his head. "No. That money's been filtered away, possibly into a new name and into an off-shore account. You can bet your bottom dollar that the wife knows where it is."

Bill made another note in his notebook. "The questions just keep coming," he said sorrowfully.

"So what is this homonym thing then?" asked Eve. "I've never heard the word."

"Basically," said Adam, "it's a word that sounds the same, but has a different meaning. They can be spelt the same or as in the case of South, on the phone, totally different."

"Chicken," said South. "That's a good one." He flapped his arms and clucked. "Or someone can be a chicken or you can chicken out of doing something."

"Wine is another one," interrupted Adam. "You can drink wine or have a good old whine. There's thousands of homonyms in the English language, Eve."

"And you think Zach's last words were some sort of homonym? So 'his call' could in fact be another word all together?" observed Eve.

"Precisely," Adam agreed.

 So chicken and chicken. Wine and whine. Mentor and mental. Cycle path and psychopath. What about bear and bear? That must be a true homonym because that's spelt the same, but has two different meanings."

They all laughed. "Now you are getting the hang of it, Eve," smiled Adam. "The trouble is that we have to bring James into the equation. Was 'his call' what he actually heard? And more importantly, if Zach did know who his killer was, how did he know? If the Reverend is to be believed and Zach was asleep and the killer shot him from his right? What did Zach see in the moment before he was shot? Did he wake up at the last moment, turn his head to his right and catch a glimpse of someone? It was a hot day. The sun was blazing. He would have been drowsy and bleary eyed. What was so distinctive about the killer, that Zach knew who he or she was?"

Andy placed his hands on the top of his head and stretched. He blew out a sigh. "So many questions and not an answer to one," he moaned. He looked at South who was writing everything in his notebook. "Hopefully we can get the answers tomorrow. Tonight I'm whacked. I think we'll take ourselves off and go back to the hotel. We have enough to deal with for the time being. I expect South and I will be up all night trying to find a solution. You know the old saying, Dad. The longer it takes…"

"The more time the murderer has to cover his tracks,"

Adam finished.

The three men stood up. Eve went to follow but was waved back into her seat. "You stay there, Eve and finish your wine. I'll see these boys out."

So Eve sat and relaxed against the back of the chair. She tilted her head to the sky, still a vivid blue and thought deeply. What had Zach meant? she wondered. What had he seen? She placed the four suspects in her head. Felicity walking over the coastal path. Michael sitting on the cliff top. Jennifer in the cove and last of all, but definitely not least unfortunately, Julian sat alone and unnoticed in his car. In her own head she discounted Felicity and her son so that left Michael and Jennifer. One had denied going into the cove, the other said that Zach was asleep. Yet if Zach saw Jennifer kill him how did the words equate. 'His call' and Jennifer bore no resemblance whatsoever. Unless... Eve sat up straight and concentrated. She imagined Zach sat in the deckchair, his murderer moving out of eye shot. Maybe he heard a noise, a crunch on the pebbles. He sees his murderer, the glint of the gun in the sunlight. He faces forward, rises from the deckchair for a confrontation and bang. Too late.

And then dying, his damaged brain trying to make sense. 'His call' his final words on his lips. But that's impossible, Eve decided. That didn't make any sense at all. She came aware of Adam moving beside her, the clinking of the glass as he refilled her wine. As if aware of her concentration he remained silent, but an idea began to form in her tired mind. She stared at him directly as he lounged back and watched her. "I think I know who did it," she stated. "I don't know how Zach realised but it could have been the clothes that he recognised. It would have happened in seconds. The sun was glaring down, bouncing off the cliff and shining into his face. When he saw the gun he must have tried to sit up and face his killer but by then it was too late."

Adam looked unconvinced. "But what about his words to James? 'His call', where does that fit into the equation?"

"Well if you let me explain. To my mind it's perfectly

plausible, but be honest and tell me what you think." She put her elbows on the table and took a sip of wine and then a deep breath. "Well here goes and no interruptions until I've finished," she warned. And so she told him her deductions and whilst she talked she noted Adam's attention becoming more alert as he digested the information. Finally, when she had finished and looked at him hopefully, he smiled and nodded.

"I think you could be right, Eve. Okay the timings a bit out and the killer had a lot of luck and the things about the clothes are a bit far-fetched, but I see where you're coming from. The most important brainwave on your part was his last words. It has to be right. What dying man says 'his call'? I'd stake my life that you're on the right track." He got out of the chair. "I'm going to phone Andy and run it by him." He walked away then doubled round and leant over her chair. He kissed her soundly on the lips. "Well done, Mrs Traversy." And walked back into the cottage, leaving Eve with a huge contented smile on her face.

Chapter Eleven

Monday morning appeared, dull, drab and humid. A teasing breeze buffeted the trees, but did little to dispel the claustrophobic heat that loitered with spiteful intent in the room. DCI Fortune's office was small compared to the other rooms in the building which were used mainly by constables, sitting behind computer terminals and even the detainee suites boasted a modern air conditioning unit, and more room. God forbid the inmates suffer, Andy thought maliciously. Here in Dorset there was no luxury of air conditioning in his office and the small unit that was supposed to blast out cold air sat redundant in the corner of the room, long broken and past repair. The smell of dried seaweed wafted through the open window and left a vague salty imprint on the two men's lips adding to their discomfort as they pored over their paperwork.

Andy stretched, hating the way his clothes clung to his skin as if he'd just stepped out of a shower and forgotten to dry himself. Muttering under his breath he slumped untidily at his desk, tired and irritable after a sleepless night. He finally got up and paced restlessly. After his father's call the night before, he and South had spent hours poring over statements, trying to find that elusive mistake that most killers make. The conclusion that only Mrs Allington or her son Michael could have been the killer lingered irresolutely in their minds.

South spoke absentmindedly. "Although I see where Mrs Traversy is coming from, sir, I still don't see how Michael Allington could have fired that shot. He was sat on the other side of the beach on top of the cliff. He saw our Reverend go into the cove just after twelve, let's say ten past twelve by the time he reached our victim. Mrs Allington said in her statement that the Reverend hesitated for quite a while before going in. The Reverend also admits to dithering in the area, probably trying to work up the courage to have this so-called chat with the victim," South said dubiously. "Now assuming the helicopter muted the sound of the gun being fired and it took him another ten minutes to climb up the cliff face and disappear unobserved from the cove, this takes us to about twelve twenty-five, give or take a couple of minutes. Now Michael Allington by his own admission didn't notice his stepmother following the Reverend, he was apparently lying down." He paused for breath and took a sip of his now cold tea. He grimaced and gave the mug an accusatory glance. He put the mug back down on his desk, noting that his boss was listening intently. He checked his notes. "Now, again allowing Mrs Allington the same amount of time and taking into account that blasted helicopter, the earliest she could have got out of the cove is about twelve thirty. James Allington, being of some sound mind checked his watch immediately his father died and that was about twelve forty-five, which in fact corresponds with the coroner's report. Now I know we've been through this, it feel like at least a hundred times, but on that timescale, there is no way Michael Allington could have climbed down the cliff, crossed the beach, entered the cove, shot his father without a shot being heard, remembering that the blasted helicopter had flown off by then, and climbed out of the cove without being seen."

Andy's sigh was audible. He pulled out a clean hanky and wiped his brow. "This is ridiculous," he said with ill humour. "I know you're right, South, yet I also know that Eve Traversy's right as well." He shook his head. His thick hair didn't move, it clung so damply to his skull. "Yet it's the weirdest homonym I've ever heard." He banged his fist on the desk in frustration. "But it fits, South. It fits perfectly, and given Zach Allington's pedantic nature and his penchant for emphasizing his family's names in full, and the added fact that he was dying and struggling to say anything, it must be correct."

"But how did the victim know, sir? What was it that caught his eye, that he could make such a positive identification?"

"Blast if I know," Andy admitted begrudgingly. "Dad and Eve reckon it must have been their clothes." He frowned. "Just out of curiosity. What were they both wearing on that day?"

South consulted his notebook and then after a few moments reshuffling his paperwork he looked up with a brightening smile. "Well, well," he said in a deep voice. "Mrs Traversy may have a point, sir." He stood up and the two men bent over Andy's desk. South pointed with his finger. "Michael Allington was wearing white T-shirt and matching shorts, socks and trainers, and look here. Mrs Allington was wearing a white cardigan and pale blue shorts. Apparently she got badly burnt on her shoulders the day before and slipped on the cardigan before she left the house. Every time we've seen Michael, he's been wearing that sort of tennis attire, and remember when we interviewed Mrs Allington on the Saturday, she kept pulling the cardigan over her shoulders because it kept slipping."

Andy sat down again and chewed on his little finger. "So what we're saying, South, is that because Michael always seems to wear white, Zach Allington assumed that he was the one that fired the gun, when in fact, we believe he caught a glimpse of his wife and it was she who was holding the gun."

"And because James is a bit simple like, he misinterpreted his father's words," South said.

"Absolutely," Andy agreed. He had an idea. "I'll tell you what, South. Let's try an experiment. Go and get a constable for me and bring him in here."

South left on his errand and Andy went and stood by the open window. Traffic on the coast road was minimal this time in the morning and bar the rustle of the trees at the end of the drive, all was silent. A few puffy white clouds meandered across a lack-lustre blue sky, but over the tree tops and out towards the horizon, a grey haze moved slowly towards the coastline. Hopefully the threat of rain would turn into a promise because he didn't think he could stand the clammy assault on his body for much longer. The thought of stripping off and plunging under a cold shower again filled him with longing, but it was barely seven in the morning, the beginning of what was going to be a very long day. Sometimes he yearned for London where the humidity rarely lowered to street level and air conditioning was the norm in most offices.

South came back preceding a reluctant Constable Collins who looked as drained and miserable as Andy felt. His thin dark hair, greying slightly at the temples lay flat, the hairs gluing themselves together, exposing a rapidly balding skull. Sweat gleamed on his forehead and he struggled to stay still before the desk. He wore the regulation uniform, heavy boots and dark trousers and a tight fitting Lycra tunic which shaped his body. Over the top he wore his tactical vest which Andy knew, having been in uniform many years before, weighed at least two and a half stone. Add to that the numerous deep pockets which homed pencils, pads, radio, mobile and other assorted paraphernalia, each officer was carrying a heavy load. Each man and woman knew however how essential it was to them to wear the correct gear, even the Community Patrol Officers and Special Constables were equipped to protect their vital organs from attack. Andy looked at Collins wilting in the heat. "Take your vest off, Collins," he instructed. "I have a little play acting for you."

Collins groaned but removed his vest gratefully and placed it on the chair. "I hope it's not role playing, sir. I hate doing that," he grumbled.

"Stop moaning, man," South berated. "Now go and sit in the chief's chair and play dead or pretend you are dying which would be better.

The constable sighed deeply but obeyed. He lay back against the headrest facing away from the window. "Right, Collins. We'll pretend you are in the cove. The sun is blazing down and you're half asleep. You hear something that wakes you up, turn your head and look over your right shoulder. You see someone, so turn your head forward again and make to rise from the chair. The gun fires and you slump back." Collins did as instructed and his head lolled back. "Now," Andy continued. "You're dying. Your senses are leaving you and then, for whatever reason, James Allington clambers down the cliff and walks over to you. South, you play James. Let's assume he leans over you and stares into your face. You can feel his presence and you try to tell him who shot you. Now, Collins. It's your last breath. You have very little time left. You start to speak and your final words come out in a gasp."

"His… call," Collins said dramatically. He frowned and sat forward. "That doesn't make sense, sir."

South pushed him back. "Close your eyes, man. We haven't finished yet."

"I want you, Collins, to go through the names of our suspects starting from the Peacefuls and work your way through the family."

"Okay, sir. Let's see. There was Ian Peaceful. Muriel Peaceful. Miss Battersby. Percy Crouch."

"Now the family but just their full first names," said Andy. "And pronounce their names slowly."

Collins complied hesitantly. "Jen…ni…fer. Fel…ic…ity. Ju…li…an. Ja…mes. Mic…hael." He frowned. "Michael. Michael." Collins sat up. "My God, sir. I get it. Zach Allington didn't say 'his call'. He said 'my call' or better still. Michael."

Andy explained in more detail. "Exactly, Collins. I think when he was dying and his words were coming out slowly, he had to split his son's name. Hence 'My'… then we can assume he gasped for breath, 'call' and James, when trying to tell us, put his own interpretation on those words, and assumed his father was admitting it was 'his call'. It was all this God thing that confused us all. We wrongly thought that Zach Allington had some sort of vision and was admitting it was his fault to die. He thought he saw his son holding the gun in that last moment, before the shot was fired."

"Thought, sir?" Collins asked confused. "Why accuse his

son if it wasn't him?"

South explained about the clothes. "And take into account our victim's sleepy state and the sun bouncing off the cliff face, he could easily have been mistaken. Michael Allington wears white most of the time but this day Zach's wife, Jennifer, was also wearing light colours."

"So we're saying that it was the missus that killed him then, sir?" he asked confused. "So we're going to believe Michael Allington's statement that he didn't go to see his father in the cove?"

Andy tapped his fingers on the desk. "It looks that way."

Just then a sharp rap came on the door and Townsend stepped into the room. "Sorry to disturb you," he said sending a puzzled look at Collins sat in the chief's chair and the two detectives standing over him. "But we've just had a call from a Doctor Ellis, another locum at that posh clinic in Harley Street the Allington's frequent. He's sending us a confirming email, but it seems that although our victim had a clean bill of health, Mrs Allington has a serious problem. Some sort of cancer. I'm not sure what type but she needs urgent medical attention. Apparently our victim knew the details and was supposed to take his wife for immediate treatment. They've had no word from either since."

"When did Zach find out this information?" Andy asked urgently.

Townsend consulted a piece of paper. "Two weeks ago last Saturday, sir."

"So that explains his epiphany. He finds out his wife could die without treatment yet he holds off. Why? What knowledge does he have that he would rather put his wife's life at risk? It seems to me, it's as if he's giving her a chance to redeem herself. Hence the party." Andy mulled it over walking over to the window, staring unseeingly ahead. "But from what we've heard his decision to change his life was brought on, first by his meeting with his doctor and second by his confrontation with Julian Traversy. And, of course, the decision to tell his wife was overridden by her attitude over that last two weeks. By all accounts they've been rowing incessantly."

South snorted. "What type of man holds off from telling his wife she has cancer for crying out loud?"

"I agree, South. There has to be something else. Something she has done that affected his decision."

"Maybe she knows more about that lottery ticket than she's letting on," Collins suggested tentatively.

"Or. That it was her that killed Clive Traversy," suggested South.

"Good grief, South. You could be right. We only assumed it was Zach Allington, but if I remember rightly, both he and his wife left the room for some considerable time. Collins, get on to records and get me a transcript about Mr Traversy's death. And, South. You and I'd better get along and see Dad and Eve." As Collins was leaving the room Andy shouted, "Get a team together and go and pick up Michael and Jennifer Allington. Put them downstairs in the suite but keep them separate. I want them out of that house. Also, while you're at it, get someone on to bank details and the will. I want every detail of their financial situation as it stands today. Get Townsend to contact that doctor as a matter of urgency. If he quibbles about patient confidentiality tell him it's a matter of life and death."

"What about the daughter and Julian Traversy?" Collins asked as the door closed behind him.

"Leave them for the time being, South. Let's get going. I want to get to Priest's Finger before the squad car."

Eve sat back in the old rattan chair, eyes closed and head raised to the sky. She sat beneath an old, grubby parasol that Adam had dug out from a cluttered shed, concealed behind a large growth of clematis. On the round wooden table sat a tray holding four mugs, milk, sugar and a pot of tea brewing. Overhead a young seagull screeched its high pitch whistle, looking for its parents. As the sun slowly rose, its golden beam flitted between the branches and sent a dappled dance across the garden. The trees rustled and the sweetness of the flowers pervaded the air. Wild foxgloves and roses lifted their heads to catch the sun's rays as it peeked through the trees.

She heard Andy's car coming up the track and called out to Adam. Minutes later the two men came into view and sat down. They offered no comment, seeing Eve there, sitting so comfortably, so early in the morning. She thought to explain then decided, at her age, accounting for her actions was extraneous. It was perfectly innocent anyway. So she smiled her greeting and calmly poured the tea and waited expectantly. Both Andy and South looked uncomfortable and she was tempted to prompt them. Fortunately Adam came out from the kitchen before she could open her mouth.

Andy watched the couple surreptitiously. His father was a grown man but it still felt strange to see him in the company of another woman. It had been many years since his mother had died. He'd been a young copper, only twenty-three, and following in his father's footsteps. The only difference between father and son then, and now, had been Andy's drive to further his career, to climb the echelons of power within the service. Yet his father looked different, more alert, happier than he had ever noticed with his mother. There was an air of familiarity between the couple almost as if they'd been together for ever. He felt a swift, sharp stab of jealously on his mother's behalf. That confused him. He was guiltily aware that he hadn't thought about her for years.

"You okay, son?" Adam asked. "You looked worried."

Andy shook himself out of his reverie and looked at South. His dark eyes drifted to Eve. She was sat up straight watching him warily, her eyes, a mahogany brown, watchful and intent. Gone was the relaxed countenance, she folded her arms protectively across her stomach. His father reached over and patted her bare arm encouragingly. "Don't worry, Eve. I'm here."

"Julian?" she asked cautiously.

Andy smiled and shook his head reassuringly. "No. He's fine as far as I am aware. No it's something else we need to discuss. Thanks to you, Eve, we've managed to build up a picture but I'm afraid it's going to come as a shock. That is, if we've got it right."

Eve gave a relieved sigh. "That's okay then. As long as my son is fine then I can handle anything else. So go on. Get on with it. Your father and I are waiting eagerly for all the information you have."

Adam laughed. "See what a bossy woman I've picked up," he joked breaking the tension and everyone breathed a little easier.

"It's not good though, Dad. This could still be upsetting for Eve."

"Don't worry about me, Andy," Eve said firmly. "I've been through a lot this last couple of years and I've manage just fine."

Andy looked to South and between the two men they explained their conclusion. When South spoke, explaining the experiment they had held this morning, Andy watched Eve, noted the changing emotions on her face and the frown that deepened on her brow. He registered the dawning realisation of her husband's possible infidelity, the sadness as they talked about her late husband, and then the disappointment, the disbelief. Her hand played nervously through her hair and her eyes darkened as they stared ahead. She listened intently until South stopped.

She looked thoughtful for some time. The three men were tense. Then she said quietly. "But how did she pass the lottery ticket off as Zach's?"

Andy grunted. "We don't know. From what we've learnt about the dead man, he didn't come across as gullible."

Eve disagreed. "Jenny was always manipulative you know. She could persuade Zach to do almost anything." She shrugged. "Perhaps she told Zach it was her ticket or something and asked him to say it was hers, that she didn't want the attention. Zach would have fallen for it. The chance to show the world he'd won all that money. He would have jumped at the chance." She shook her head. "He was so foolish sometimes."

"And do you think it's possible that your husband and Jennifer were having an affair?" Adam asked this time.

They heard her indrawn breath. Rubbing a finger over her lips she said, "It's possible I suppose. There were a few times. I caught them flirting together in the office many a time, but I didn't think anything of it. I mean they did spend a lot of time together. Towards the end it was Zach that did the more hands-on work whilst Clive spent a lot of time on the phone trying to drum up business. It was a very difficult time and tensions were running high. Clive and I were under a lot of stress. If the business failed we stood to lose everything. The house was mortgaged up to the hilt."

"And the Allingtons? Were they in the same position?"

"Oh yes," confirmed Eve. "I think Zach and Jenny were going through a bit of a bad patch as well, although I don't know any details. Of course, the money changed all that."

"What is Mrs Allington like, as a person I mean?" Andy asked.

"I'm probably the worst person to ask. I never particularly liked her especially during the time before Wendy died. Jenny was a terrible flirt and as I've already told you, I thought she and Zach were having an affair a long time before Wendy was killed. But then, of course, nothing happened for about eighteen months, so I dismissed it as part of my overactive imagination. And then they announced they were going to get married right out of the blue. As you know they had Felicity and seemed relatively happy, I suppose."

"Can you describe Clive's behaviour in the months leading to his death?" Andy asked.

"Well, obviously he was depressed. The thought of losing the house and business put a great deal of strain on him and he did spend a lot of time alone. Sometimes he would come home late. His excuse was that he was trying to keep the business afloat. Sometimes he didn't come home at all. He told me he slept in the office and I didn't question him because he could be so volatile. You have no idea how tense the atmosphere was at home then."

"What about the night he died? Was there anything different? Did he say or do anything that was out of character?"

Again Eve took her time in answering. Her mind went back to that night. Finally she began talking softly. "He'd been a bit agitated most of the day long before we went to dinner. I didn't want to go. I didn't enjoy their company but Clive seemed to be on a bit of a high. He was excited and furtive at the same time if you know what I mean. I thought it would cause another argument if I refused to go, so I wasn't in the best frame of mind that day."

Andy leant forward and put his elbows on the table. He looked directly into her eyes. He'd inherited his father's unassuming manner, neither man had ever used anger to illicit a confession. They asked the questions then sat back leaving the person at the other end of the investigation time and personal space. The soft, non-aggressive stance had worked for Andy throughout his police career. "Now think carefully, Eve," he said. "That night. The weather was bad. You said that Zach was out of the room making phone calls. James, Michael and Felicity were around but you didn't see them. At some point after dinner Jennifer left the room to go and make coffee, but you said in your statement, written for the inquest, that Jennifer spilt liquid on her clothes and she was away from the room for some time."

Eve nodded. "Yes I think that's right so far."

"Now where was Clive during this time?"

Eve concentrated, trying to focus her thoughts. "We'd finished dinner and all four of us were sitting around the table. I can't remember if the phone rang calling Zach away from the table or whether he said he was going to make a call. I'm sorry to sound so vague but it feels such a long time ago."

"You're doing fine, Eve," Adam assured. "Now just take it slowly and try to get the events of the evening into order. What happened next?"

"Well. Neither Jenny nor Clive were saying much. It was a bit strained really and then Zach came back into the room. He sat down and if my memory serves me right he was just about to talk to Clive, when Clive got up, muttering about needing some fresh air and walked out of the room. I remember feeling embarrassed and it left everyone feeling uncomfortable. For all Clive's faults I'd never known him be so socially rude. It was quite a shock."

"What happened then?" someone interrupted.

The wind was howling then and it was pouring with rain. It was thrashing against the window. That's why none of us heard the car start up and Clive drive away. I just assumed he was standing by the back door or something. Zach started talking, heaven knows what about. I think he was just trying to fill in the silence. After a few minutes Jenny left to make coffee and then a short while later the telephone rang. I heard it that time. Zach apologised and left the room and then Jenny popped her head round the door and said she'd spilt coffee on her clothes and was just going to pop upstairs." Eve sat back in the chair and feathered her hands through her hair. "And the rest you know," she concluded dully.

Andy looked thoughtful. "How long were you alone?"

"Well it didn't feel long. I went to look out of the window a couple of times. I was worried about Clive and couldn't settle. So all in all, I suppose about fifteen to twenty minutes."

"Who came back first?"

"Zach did. He said it was a business call. He'd managed to find work from a local contractor which would bring in enough work to tide them over. He looked very pleased with himself."

"And Jennifer?"

"Oh she was ages, but that's Jenny for you."

"Did she look flustered or anything when she got back?"

Eve shook her head. "Not really. Not that I noticed anyway but you have to remember that my mind was full of Clive. I was worried that he'd gone off somewhere and left me alone." She looked guilty. "I hate admitting this but at the time I was very angry. I felt humiliated and stupid sat there. Nobody mentioned Clive for ages and then suddenly Zach said he was going to look for him. Five minutes later he came back, soaked through. He could find no sign of Clive or his car. We waited nearly an hour and it was then that I phoned home and spoke to Julian and of course he'd seen nothing of his father."

"Who decided to call the police? After all he was a grown man."

"It was me. Clive's actions were so out of character. I know he'd been acting strange for some time but I had this bad feeling and insisted Zach phone the police."

After a short silence Adam spoke, looking towards Eve apprehensively. She was obviously upset and he was surprised to find himself hurting on her behalf. "So do you think, like us, that it could have been Jennifer that pushed Clive off the cliff?"

Andy said. "It all fits. Perhaps... and I hate to be so brutal, Eve, but maybe your husband and Mrs Allington arranged to meet to discuss the lottery win? Clive showed her the ticket, she saw her opportunity, pushed him and ran back to the house. The excuse that she had to change her clothes was probably premeditated. I'm presuming that she knew about the win, and if Clive was smitten with her she could easily have arranged for him to wait at the top of the cliffs. A quick push and it was over. All she had to do then was to walk casually back into the room. She could have been there and back in fifteen minutes."

Eve buried her face in her hands. "Oh how callous. And poor Clive. He must have died terrified. He hated heights. She knew it too, so how could she be so cruel? Why didn't she and Clive just run off with each other?"

170

"Mrs Allington doesn't seem the type of woman who likes to share," South said seriously. "She was greedy and if it meant staying with her husband, then so be it. There was a hell of a lot of money at stake and if she'd stayed with Clive, she would have had to share it with you."

Eve wrapped her arms around her body. She was suddenly very cold. "She would never have done that."

"And after Julian visited Zach and confronted him with the rest of the tickets, Zach must have grasped what had happened and decided to hold a party. Perhaps he finally realised just what sort of person she really was. Maybe he didn't like the person he saw in the mirror. He'd only just found out how seriously ill his wife was, and I think he was giving her a chance to confess. Hence the letter to you, Eve. He was trying to make amends, not only to you, but to the Peacefuls, Miss Battersby and Mr Crouch, and of course Julian."

"I think you're right. But we'll never have proof will we? Zach's dead and his thoughts and feelings died with him. Jennifer must have realised the game was up, hence the need to get rid of Zach as quick as possible. She couldn't wait until the party, yet she took a big risk. Zach or I could easily have gone looking for her the night she killed Clive and any one of the family and neighbours could have caught her shooting Zach in the cove."

South looked up. "She was desperate, wasn't she? And if it hadn't been for you, Eve, deciphering that puzzle of Zach Allington's last words, this case could have gone unsolved for ever."

"Just get her to confess. That will be enough for the moment," Eve said ruthlessly.

Chapter Twelve

It was twelve thirty in the morning and there was uproar in the station. Officers were rushing around, waving papers and talking on phones. Andy and South were cosseted in their office listening to a barrage of complaints from an angry Chief Constable. Her face was hard and unyielding. She was clearly unhappy and it showed in the way her voice roared. "You've lost all your suspects?" she asked disbelievingly. "All five of them?"

"Three actually," South said daringly. "Felicity and Julian Traversy have been apprehended in Bridport. They're being questioned by Collins and Townsend downstairs right now. It's the other three we can't find."

Chief Constable Diane Brace slammed her palm down heavily on the desk. It must have hurt but she didn't flinch. "Have you put out an all-points bulletin, Fortune, or have you forgotten?" she added sarcastically.

"Everything is under control, ma'am. The bulletin has gone out to all ports and airports. And my men are scouring the area around Priest's Finger. They can't have gone far," he said with more assurance than he felt. He looked out of the window. The threatened rain had finally put in an appearance. The atmosphere in the small room simmered with anger and failure. A fluorescent strip light hummed above on the off-white ceiling sending a murky brown aurora around its edge. The rain had brought heavy low grey clouds, which swirled around in the sky. Yesterday's summer had become today's autumn and the air of doom and gloom in the room matched the forbidden sky. Andy reread the doctor's report. Mrs Allington was indeed lucky. Early detection of pancreatic cancer gave her a good chance of survival. "If they could find her quickly enough," he muttered to himself. With such a cancer, silent and symptomless until it was too late, it was literately a matter of life and death. But for the moment, she had disappeared off the radar. And James and Michael Allington? Where the hell had they gone? He hardly thought that they had left with their stepmother. Even he, a stranger, had felt the hostile friction that frizzled between them. He suspected she'd packed her bags and made for a sunnier climate and she must have left sometime early last evening to give her a chance to get out of sight. She wouldn't stay in England, he surmised. Andy wouldn't be surprised if she'd already left this country. He had no doubts now that she was a murderer though. A cold, callous killer.

With a sharp rap on the door Collins entered the room. The Chief Constable gave him a stern look. "What is it, Constable?" she asked brusquely.

"We've got some information from Heathrow Airport, ma'am."

"And?" she said impatiently.

Collins faltered. He'd been an officer for ten years and this was the first time such a senior officer had been in this building. He looked hesitantly towards DCI Fortune. "Mrs Allington, sir. Her car has been found in Heston Services on the M4 and it seems like someone bearing her description took the zero five twenty flight to Spain. The passport was registered in the name of Jennifer Alison Golding. That's the suspect's maiden name. We've been in contact with the Spanish side, but not a lot of hope there, sir. The plane landed in Alicante about nine o'clock their time. They've put out a bulletin but they don't sound too hopeful of a sighting. It's high tourist season and the place is packed with holiday makers. It'll be like looking for a needle in a haystack," he finished morosely.

The Chief Constable sighed dramatically. "That will be all, Constable." As Collins left the room she turned to Andy. "Well. Her capture is out of our hands for the moment. Let's hope there's better news on the home front."

Andy acknowledged her statement pessimistically. "For her own sake I hope they find her soon," he said under his breath.

They found Michael and James a few hours later. James, finally reaching his own conclusion about his father's death had lured Michael from his bed in the early hours of the morning. Jennifer had left long before but it was the sound of her car stirring up the gravel on the drive that had awoken James, leaving him in the darkness to mull over the conundrum of his father's last words.

Although Michael was reluctant to leave the house, his brother's urgent words and ranting syllables about a killer on the cliffs had seen him dress drowsily and trudge across the skyline with an excited James leading the way. A heated argument had ensued with James throwing out accusations. In a rash, violent move he had pushed his brother over the edge. Fortunately the tide had been in and the sea water calm. Battered and bruised and in a great deal of pain Michael had clambered on to the exposed rocks and hauled himself to shelter in a small cave. His shouts had gone unheeded, and James, simple and afraid, had kept a silent vigil on top of the cliff. There he had lain, curled up in a ball and slept the rest of the night away. When the sun rose and glittered on a flat sea he had woken sluggishly, raised heavy eyelids and completely forgotten about his brother. He stumbled across the coast path and went and sat in the cove where his father breathed his last. And there he was found, staring out into the distance, happy and content in his own little world.

It was another hour before they found Michael. James' incoherent mutterings had finally led them to the top of the cliff and the officers' calls were finally answered by weak cries from the rocks below.

Michael Allington spent three days in Dorchester hospital. His wounds were superficial, fortunately for him nothing was broken. His life was in tatters though. No home, friends and importantly, no more money. He went back to the manor and after intensive questioning was finally cleared by the police of any offence regarding his father's death. Fliss and Julian wrote him a cheque, which he took resentfully and without thanks, hating them both, but in no position to refuse the money. By the time he'd paid his debts and found himself somewhere to live, there would be little left for any of the luxuries he was used to. He left the manor early one evening, slinking out the door and carrying one large used suitcase. With no goodbyes and without a backward glance, he got in his car and drove away. He gave no thought to his stepmother's serious medical condition other than wishing he could be a fly on the wall when she found out. Too late he hoped, to get anything more than palliative care at the end of her life. Or a tranquilizer gun, he sometimes thought to himself with a smirk.

Felicity and Julian decided to stay on at the manor, even though Priest's Finger held no happy memories for either of them. They elected to remain and stamp their own impression on the house. Without her mother's influence Felicity had managed to curb that part of her more melodramatic nature, and took on the house with renewed vigour. Julian carried on working even though they were rich enough that he never had to work again. With help they also invested a large amount of money for their future. Jennifer had managed to filter more than half of the lottery win, the majority they found out, which also confirmed the police conclusion, within weeks of the money being put into Zach and her joint account.

Eve visited infrequently. She wisely wanted the newly-weds to make their own mark and get used to each other, and partly because she still wasn't sure how to interact with Felicity, unsure whether the girl resented her influence over her new husband. A large settlement had come to Eve almost immediately, courtesy of her son, but Eve refused to take any more than she needed, even though her son insisted it was really her money. She had no need for such an amount and at the end of the day, she explained to them, whatever money she had, would end up with her son anyway. The only objection she had, and it was a silent objection, was the decision by Julian and Felicity to keep James with them.

James Allington was put into a special unit at an exclusive care home on the edge of the New Forest whilst, at great expense, an annex was built on the side of the manor. For the time being though he settled in the home and resided in blissful ignorance, happy to have his own space and the peace and quiet he craved. No tension, no anger, no noise, and kind people who cared for him and kept him company in the large grounds. His only recollection of his father was of a lonely man sat on a deckchair in a small cove. Of Jennifer, he gave not a passing thought. The rest of the family lived on the perimeter of his mind, shadowy figures who brought anxious feelings when they intruded, even for a short moment, into his mind. As he settled, he began regarding the sprawling building as his home. No one had the heart to tell him, that soon, in the near future, he would have to go back to the house that held so much torment to him.

No charges were drawn against him, and given his state of mind, prosecution was never considered. In a rare moment of goodness, Michael Allington defended his younger brother, understanding the agitation of his mind.

For the people straying within the boundary of murder, life went on, but not quite as normal. Muriel Peaceful packed her meagre belongings in bags one day and walked away from her husband. She did this without regret and withdrew every penny from their joint account. It was her money after all, although her husband would doubtless refute that. But she didn't care. Time for her life now, without the shackles of marriage. Muriel made her way to Hammersmith where she'd been most happiest, quickly connecting with old friends. She made herself busy joining knitting clubs and the WI. If she thought about Ian, which wasn't often, she pictured him as a black cloud that had once surrounded her, but thankfully gone now and easily forgotten. Independence came quickly bringing with it a comfort she hadn't experienced for a very long time.

Whilst his wife embraced her new found freedom the Reverend Ian Peaceful brooded. He remained in the house in Priest's Finger, closeting himself away and surrounding himself with books and writings. He felt self-righteously dejected and endlessly obsessed about his absent wife. She'd never manage without him, he thought to himself constantly. The woman clearly needed a strong man to control her life and her money. Every day he waited for Muriel to walk through the door, submissive and contrite at the terrible affliction she had put on her husband. Ian imagined the scenario over and over again. The thought of her grovelling was the only thing that brought a cruel smile to his lips. He'd stand at the end of the room, his magisterial bearing silhouetted against the window and stare out towards the gate. He imagined himself being magnanimous and gracious as he opened the door and issued her into the gloomy interior. She would be so grateful, he thought, but he'd make her suffer. Of that you could be sure.

Jennifer Allington was another matter altogether. The woman had played him for a fool and her actions left an unsavoury taste in his month. That he entered the cove, a knife concealed on his person with the intent to kill a man, rarely, if ever intruded on his thoughts. He'd probably have left Muriel for her but at the end of the day it was her loss. So, Ian Peaceful waited all the days long.

Four weeks to the day that Zach Allington lost his life, Miss Battersby, spinster of the parish, sat in her chair by the open grate and sipped her Horlicks. Before retiring she had secured the doors, turned everything off in the kitchen, put on her faithful linen nightie and wrapped the heavy dressing gown around her. On to her feet she slipped an old pair of tartan slippers. Her routine was comfortable and reliable. Basically, she was a creature of habit and at exactly eight o'clock every night, after following this ritual, she would relax in her chair.

The inclement weather and brooding sky brought a dingy gloom into the small room and without television or radio the silence was complete and forbidding. She stared ahead, her eyes pale, lifeless and unseeing. Her gnarled hands rested primly on her lap. Death brought her no warning. The Horlicks beside her on the little coffee table gradually cooled and congealed leaving a thick film of soggy skin on its surface. The corpse, frail in life as it now was in death remained strait laced in the hard, upright seat.

Life was easy and sunny for Alison Golding aka Jennifer Allington. First she had pottered around Spain, mingling with the throng of holiday makers before swapping countries and travelling unmolested around the rest of Europe. Finally feeling safe from the authorities and confident with her new look she returned to Spain and set up home in the little town of Moriara, in a large villa overlooking the warm sea. It never worried her that she would be recognised. She dyed her hair back to its original colour, an almond brown and wore coloured contact lenses. She was able to walk anonymously among the ex-pats without concern.

Alison aka Jennifer made a point of not getting too involved with the English people. She was always distantly polite and deliberately turned her eyes away from any English newspapers or magazines. Life was good. Carlos, one of a string of young men who kept her company, lay lounging beside the swimming pool. His firm tanned body drew her eyes, his muscles flexed as he stretched. He was quite happy not to delve into the English woman's life. She had money and lots of it and her generosity was very appealing. Her age was irrelevant. When you now wore a Rolex watch and had a wardrobe full of expensive clothes then you could turn a blind eye to the more obvious flaws of this strange English woman.

Jennifer knew exactly what Carlos saw when he looked at her. A gullible woman, a euphemism for a cash cow but she didn't care. He was pretty to look at and between the sheets he gave her a great deal of pleasure. And, besides, when she tired of him there were plenty more fish in the sea. Plenty of young men to decorate her pool and none that she would ever need to be beholden to. It was such a pleasing thought.

She lay back in the lounger and stared out to the sparkling sea. The sky was cobalt blue, the sea a deep aquamarine. Children screamed and played on the water's edge and a lonely plane flew overhead. Her bank account was overloaded with cash. She had so much and needed no one. Her smile was wide and self-congratulatory. This was the life, she thought exultantly. One day she might move on but now was not the time to think about the future. She got up and sashayed over to the pool. Carlos lifted his glasses exposing lovely black eyes. He smiled invitingly and moved over on the lounger. She lay down beside him and welcomed the soft caress of his hands. After all, she mused, she had all the time in the world.

Six weeks after the death of Zach Allington, Adam and Eve returned to Dorset. They rented a little cottage on the edge of the village of Portesham. Here, nestled in the heart of the village, was the home of Thomas Hardy, the sea captain who held Admiral Nelson in his arms when he died. Their cottage sat farther up the hill nearer Hardy's monument positioned proudly on the hilltop overlooking the Dorset countryside and the sea around Weymouth. They revisited old haunts but steered clear of Priest's Finger. Fliss and Julian were away, holidaying abroad somewhere.

In a few hours Adam and South were coming to dinner but for now the couple wandered hand in hand on the beach at Abbotsbury. They had discussed the murder a lot over the past few weeks, so much so, that the shock of Zach and Clive's death gradually faded into the back of her mind. "I wonder what Andy wants?" she said thoughtfully. "He seemed quite insistent that we come back to Dorset. Not that I'm bothered to be back," she assured Adam. "It's a beautiful county."

Adam stared out into the ocean. Nearing the end of September the air was cooling rapidly. Gone was the sultry days of August. Now the sea was restless and storm clouds loomed in the distance. A fresh wind ruffled their hair as they strolled along the pebbles. "I suppose we'd better make our way back," Adam said reluctantly.

Eve squeezed his hand. "Come on, Adam. I know you're itching to find out what your son wants. Perhaps he's found Jenny."

He shook his head. "I don't think so. He'd hardly arrange a meeting and drag us down here if she's been found. He could have told me that on the phone."

"I agree, but I am intrigued. Aren't you?"

Adam laughed heartily and squeezed her hand. "Yes," he admitted. "I'm very interested and you know it."

"Great minds think alike," Eve replied. She was really happy and knew it was because of the man who walked beside her. They'd developed a bond gelled by conspiracy. They were both nosy, liked to delve into people's lives, their relationship thrived on the mystery of other human being. Where there were problems and mysteries, there was Adam and Eve in the thick of it. Tentatively, they agreed that maybe they might start up a detective agency somewhere in the heart of the West Country. A discreet office, off the beaten track, away from prying eyes. A discreet service provided by two wise and intelligent private investigators. Adventure beckoned.

Eve thought it was a great idea. Okay, she had a lot to learn but Adam was a good and patient teacher. With Zach's murder she had been on the periphery of the investigation but she realised during the course of the investigation that she had an eye for detail and recall. She was a good listener and she had an enquiring mind. With Adam's knowledge they'd make a great team. She was very happy that Adam felt the same. What Andy would say was a different matter but one they would put off until another time.

DCI Andy Fortune and DS South turned up at the cottage in full police mode. Before dinner had been placed on the table, Andy pulled out an envelope from his inside pocket. He reached over and placed it beside Eve's hand. She looked enquiringly first at the long white envelope then at Andy. "What is this?" she asked.

Andy had an interrogative look in his eyes. South remained silent, watching. Andy said, "This arrived three days ago, hand delivered by a clerk for solicitors Birchwood and Watson in Cheapside, London. They have been trying to trace you for some time but I explained that you were roaming around England with my father. After much deliberation they agreed that I should be the one to hand it to you."

Eve picked up the envelope and turned it over in her hands. She recognised the writing on the front. She gave a confused look around the table. "It's from Zach?"

Andy nodded. "We know. That was the only thing the clerk would divulge. It seems he handed this letter to his solicitors a week before he died with the express wish that should anything happen to him, you should receive this letter. It took five weeks to reach me." He looked at her steadily. "Aren't you going to read it?"

Eve looked at Adam and then back to his son. "Your father and I will go into the other room and read it in private if you don't mind, Andy."

DCI Fortune had no choice but to agree. "Will you let me read it when you finish please? It could be more evidence and may provide answers. There are still a few loose ends."

Adam pulled Eve's chair out and they left the room. Before the door closed Adam said over his shoulder. "Help yourself to beer, lads. We won't be long. It's spaghetti bolognese for dinner so it won't spoil."

In the small room at the back of the cottage Eve stood uncertainly in the middle of the room. She stared at the letter for some time then heaved a sigh. She shoved the envelope towards Adam. "You read it," she said bluntly.

Adam tore open the envelope and opened up the letter. He cleared his throat.

My Dear Evangeline

If you are reading this letter then I must have died in suspicious circumstances. I've wronged you, Eve, and your son and I need to put things right so I'm going to tell you a true story. Don't worry it won't take long.

It began twenty-eight years ago. Wendy and I were going through a rough patch. Jennifer came on to me, she began flirting. At the beginning that was all there was to it. I promise you, Eve, that all the while Wendy was alive I was faithful to her but it was hard. Jennifer made her feelings for me perfectly clear. Anyway I digress. As you know Wendy was killed by a hit and run driver whilst she was walking home one night. It's strange but I always suspected Jennifer had done it, but after Wendy died Jennifer kept her distance. Suddenly it was me doing all the running and finally she consented to be my wife.

As you know all went well with our marriage and after a year we had Felicity and I was happy and content. And so we plodded on for years until the night Clive died.

Like everyone else I believed that Clive committed suicide. Times were bad then, Evangeline. Money was tight, work was scarce. I felt suicidal myself sometimes.

And then Jennifer turned up with that lottery ticket. She told me that she had won, that she didn't want the publicity and would I pretend it was me. I was shocked but you know what a greedy bastard I am don't you? I practically snapped her hands off. I was in my element. We were rich. The whole experience was incredible and I was happy lording it over my little empire until that fateful Saturday.

And then the doctor's news. Jennifer has cancer, Evangeline. Without immediate treatment she will die. I was beside myself all morning and then Julian turned up and everything fell to pieces. My world crashed. Even though I wanted to deny what your son told me I knew in my heart that he was telling the truth.

Of course I put two and two together and realised that the only way Jennifer could have got hold of that ticket was to kill Clive. It's taken me a week to write this letter but now she knows that I intend to give you the rest of the money and to beg your forgiveness next Saturday, I fear for my life, Evangeline. She's already killed twice, one more won't make a difference.

I'm sorry, Evangeline, and I leave it in your hands. It's up to you what happens next.

Adam put the letter on to the table. Eve stood before him, tears in her eyes and trickling down her face. She shook her head. "Poor Zach. Poor wonderful, stupid Zach."

Adam stepped closer and wrapped Eve in his arms. She lifted her tear stained face. She offered no resistance when Adam slowly lowered his lips on to hers. They shared their first real kiss.

South tapped lightly on the door. Receiving no answer he opened it gently. He saw the couple embrace, their lips meeting. His eyes bulged. "Well," he muttered under his breath, "Would you Adam and Eve it."

17551961R00111

Printed in Great Britain
by Amazon